Witty Carly's Wishes

(Carol Lai Ling Young)

Book design by Jansina of Rivershore Books

ISBN: 978-1-63522-029-2

Printed in the United States of America
10   9   8   7   6   5   4   3   2   1

Rivershore Books
8982 Van Buren St. NE • Minneapolis, MN 55434
763-670-8677 • info@rivershorebooks.com

This book is loosely based on a true story. Names have been changed. Some scenes are partially true, while others are the work of the author's imagination.

Chapter One

As I sit in my cosy recliner due to lack of mobility, balance, and energy, my thoughts go back seventy some years bringing me fond memories of a past era. Slowly my heavy eyelids close over my weary eyes. Drifting from a dreamlike daze into thoughts of my childhood days, I feel the fresh autumn breeze of a cool day with the sun peeking through the white, fluffy clouds. My eyes are fixed on the beautifully coloured red-and-orange leaves floating through the air, falling gently to the ground, covering the dew drops on the green grass. My ears detect the echoing sounds of children's voices and laughter in the background.

This was the last week for the kids on my block to get together, talk about their summer holiday activities, and prepare for their new school year, which was to begin in a week. I was one of the neighbourhood group. I couldn't be happier living with my large family, having lots of neighbourhood friends, and carrying on with the usual day-to-day, month-to-month, season-by-season routine and activities. Little did I know that in the near future there would be a drastic change in my life that would upset my carefree childhood days.

During those days I was a happy, active child in my large family, which consisted of one brother among four girls. Joe was a tall, lanky six-foot-two fellow with brownish blond, wavy hair and blue eyes. He bore a striking resemblance to Dad. Rather than be around his sisters who outnumbered him, he'd hang around his buddies who were more interested in snazzy cars and sports games. When he was old enough for a driver's licence, he and his friends pooled their resources and bought an old Ford that a neighbour was about to trash for a few dollars. They purchased some paint and spray painted some large black flames on the green car. The guys were hoping this one-of-a-kind vehicle might attract a few girls. The problem was that after tinkering with the car motor, the Ford conked out before it actually got started.

A year younger than Joe was a sibling named Lena who would have made a great football player with her husky-like frame. We always wanted her on our team when we played Red Rover because she would send some of the players flying if they didn't drop hands first when they saw her charging. Just two years younger than Lena was Shelley, who was a bit of a tomboy in spite of her stature. She liked playing tricks on us and Mom knew she was up to no good when we came home shrieking, being chased by someone holding up a snake, spider, or mouse. We never knew whether it was real or a rubber toy, but weren't taking any chances just in case.

Then came me, Carly, a bit on the timid, quiet side in comparison to my two older sisters, although I could be pretty stubborn and determined at times. Like most brothers and sisters, there were times when we'd have a minor squabble over something, but it would appear and disappear in the blink of an eye.

We were one big, happy family. You couldn't have asked for more loving and caring parents. By the way, Mom and Dad were not my sisters' and my biological parents; they were our foster parents. I was taken in by them when I was a baby since my Chinese mother, who was born in B.C., died when she was very young, and my father, who was born in Guangdong Province, was unable to look after me. I also didn't mention—not that it matters—that Mom and Dad who nurtured me were Caucasian; I was Chinese.

Mom was a five-foot-two, blue-eyed, medium-built woman in her forties who looked older because of her short, gray, wavy hair. She was a kind, gentle, pleasant person with many talents who always seemed to be busy. When she wasn't cooking, baking, sewing, or doing the laundry or other household chores, she'd be helping us with schoolwork or playing the piano. But then, with five kids, what mother wouldn't be busy. The odd time we girls would decide to surprise Mom and give the house a real cleaning from top to bottom. When Mom went shopping for the day, each of us would choose a room in the house to tidy up and clean so the house looked immaculate. We knew it was worth our effort when we saw the surprised look on Mom's face, the big smile, and the words of gratitude.

Dad, on the other hand, was a tall man with an average physique. He had straight, gray hair and blue eyes, and like Mom wore silver-rimmed glasses on his Germanic nose. He was skilled when it came to repairing anything that needed fixing around the house as well as doing carpentry. In the springtime, Dad would begin preparing his garden. He managed to crowd in neat rows of carrots, lettuce, beets, beans, and cabbage with room for a few potatoes. Along the side of the house was a long strip for a pea patch. Fresh garden peas were my favourite vegetable. I would open the pod and toss the peas into the air one at a time, catching them in my open mouth. Sometimes I'd scoot to the backyard when I saw Dad puttering around the backyard working in his garden, trimming the rose bushes and shrubs or cutting pieces of wood on his sawhorse. He'd look up from his task and joke with me. When I asked him if he'd like an orange, he'd smile and answer, "Sure. What kind? A drink? One that you peel? An orange what?" I knew he was just kidding again. I knew this was the beginning of one of his riddles. "When is an orange not an orange orange?" I'd think about it, then answer with, "I don't know. When is an orange not an orange?" With a chuckle, Dad would reply, "When it's a green orange. One that's not ripe." After thinking about it, the light went on in my head, and we'd both laugh. That gave me an idea. I'd wrack my brain to think of a riddle that would outsmart Dad. The next day I went to the garden where Dad was working again. Before he could utter a word, I excitedly blurted out my riddle about oranges: "When is an orange not an orange orange?" Scratching his head with a puzzled look on his face, Dad said, "You got me. It can't be a green orange. What colour is it?" Jumping up and down, I shouted, "It's a blue orange. One that's sad!" We both laughed as Dad called out, "You sure fooled me this time!" The next time Aila came over, I asked her my orange riddle, to which she couldn't respond, at least with the correct answer. After my head-scratching puzzler had made the rounds on my block, it became the fad of a new, challenging, fun game on our street.

At mealtime we had cooked meals with Dad's fresh, garden vegetables, sometimes in a stew or soup, or as a side vegetable with meat. Throughout the year I remember Dad spending time in the basement, puttering around with his tools and fixing or making things. He not only made our playhouse but built a house trailer which was often used. We thought Mom and Dad were the best parents in the whole world.

Chapter Two

I will never forget the day my natural sister, Lin, who was three years old, came to live with us. She was a cute, little tot, a bit on the thin side, with delicate facial features to match her tiny frame. We learned that she had had rheumatic fever when she was a baby, which left her with an enlarged heart. On the other hand, I was a healthy child, two years older and a few inches taller than her. In comparison to Lin, I was a chubby child with walnut-shaped eyes, a triangular, flat nose, and a small chin on my pudgy, round face. Although we both had short, straight hair, I noticed that mine was stark black while hers seemed to have a brownish tinge to it.

Taking Lin on a tour of her new home, our first stop with my new sister was on the handy register between the kitchen and dining area. The register was a welcome sight, especially after coming from outside on a cold or snowy day. The heat blowing up on our chilled bodies felt so-o-o good. Then we showed Lin the rest of the house.

It was a three-storey, brown-shingled

house, about forty years old, consisting of two bedrooms with double beds and brown, wooden dressers on the top floor. On the middle floor was a simply designed, wallpapered kitchen containing several yellow, wooden cupboards, an oval-shaped, arborite meal table sitting next to a window overlooking the large backyard, and a small, coal-burning stove to the right of a deep-set, white, porcelain kitchen sink. Next to the kitchen was an added-on room referred to as the inside porch. As we walked through this room, we recalled fond memories of our happy days with Grandpa.

When Mom's mother passed away it was decided that Grandpa would stay with us for as long as he liked. It was at that time that Dad added this room onto the house so that Mom's dad would have a comfortable place to relax and sleep. Grandpa M. was a grand, old, eighty-four year old with white hair, bushy eyebrows, and a big, white moustache that covered his kind, pleasant face. He spent hours in his rocking chair reading, humming, and sleeping. Sometimes he would tell us about his childhood days as we sat mesmerised by his stories. Other times he would teach us catchy tunes or read some of our favourite stories from our storybooks. It was a sad day when Mom told us Grandpa had gone to heaven where he was now with Grandma. Though he would be happy there, we missed him so much.

Hearing faint voices in the background of

my head, I was brought back to the reality of the moment in the inner porch. On the far side of it sat a single bed. This area led to the back door. A big smile came over Lin's face when she saw Fluffy and Toby, our two cats. Then, to her surprise she heard our beautiful, singing canary, Peter, who was perched in his hanging cage which hung from the ceiling of the inside porch. At some time or other we always had a pet or pets which were part of our family: a cat, a dog, a rabbit, a bird.

One of the pets that I remember vividly was a large, black, purebred German Shepherd named Bruno that we adopted as a puppy. When I saw this shy-looking puppy sitting quietly in a corner of the room while all the others were barking and romping about, I knew this was the cute little dog for me. He cuddled up to me, shivering in the car, not knowing what the future would hold for him. His nature seemed to change drastically a couple days after arriving home. Puppies like to chew on anything in sight and Bruno was no exception. My slippers, shoes, the corners of chairs, the top of my music hassock, and you name it were torn to shreds. When his nose was white with powder, we knew he'd been chewing on the utility wall again. We were glad he hadn't shocked himself when a broken wire was found lying on the utility room floor. In spite of his mischievous puppy episodes, as time went by, we saw a marked difference in the growing, smart, fun dog who made a loving companion. Bruno loved the sunny days when I would take him to the backyard, give his shiny coat a good brushing, and practise a few tricks. He learned to shake a paw, roll over, and understand the command "hide your head", to which he would nuzzle his head under my arm. I would toss a dog biscuit somewhere on the lawn, and, waiting anxiously for the phrase "Go and find it, Bruno," off he would dash, stopping and sniffing in various spots around the yard until he found and quickly snatched up his treat. Bruno thrived on the attention he was given by the family, not realizing he would soon be sharing this special treatment with a newcomer to our household.

Competition for our lively, lovable dog was a scrawny, black-and-white, feral kitten, which had been rescued by a worker in a large warehouse. The poor, little, starving thing was craving food and loving the care and attention he received when we were introduced to him. At first, we weren't sure how Bruno would react to a new pet in the house or how the new pet would react to a large dog like Bruno. Time would tell.

After the first few days, our new pet was named Rosco. After experiencing all his shenanigans, we tagged on "the Rascal". Rosco took to Bruno immediately and followed him everywhere probably thinking he was his mother or father, but Bruno wanted nothing to do with him and would attempt to escape by heading to another part of the house to no avail. Wherever Bruno went, Rosco went, imitating his every move. If Bruno lay on his side, Rosco would lie on his side; if Bruno rolled onto his back, Rosco would roll on to his back. Whenever Rosco attempted to cuddle up to Bruno, the poor, harassed dog would try to escape into another room. Eventually Bruno succumbed, and the two animals became friends.

Now that Bruno had outgrown his puppy stage, it was time for Rosco to show his mischievous side. No one dared to leave anything small or shiny on a table or shelf for fear that it would disappear. Watches, keys, glasses, and coins were only a few items that were found on the floor or in strange places. Flowers in vases on the dining room table were missing petals and leaves on plants had little pin marks in them. One morning it took an hour to untangle thread that had been pulled off a spool and wound around the legs of chairs and woven in and out of furniture in the dining room and living room area. Mom woke one morning to find a table on its side with pieces of a ceramic lamp strewn all over. In spite of all his episodes, when Rosco jumped up onto my knee and looked up with his big, brown, innocent eyes, all was forgiven and forgotten. Both Bruno and Rosco were part of our family, and without these two loving pets we would have been missing part of life's joys.

In our house there were two, what I call

French doors, without the window panes that separated the kitchen from the dining room which were equal in size. In the dining room was a large, dark, wooden dining table which sat on a thick, wine-coloured carpet etched with a gold rim. Against one wall was a matching buffet which stored all of Mom's special dinnerware. A dinky, dark hallway with coat hooks on one wall led to the small bathroom.

We darted across the register, passed the master bedroom into the inside porch, opened the back door, and proceeded quickly down the back staircase. As we turned to the right, there were two doors in sight. One led to the basement, which contained a furnace and working space where Dad kept his tools; the other was an extra room, which would come in handy if needed. This comfortable, old house was plenty big enough for our large family and its pets.

As youngsters, we loved to sit and listen to children's stories. I especially enjoyed the fairy tales, folk tales, and fables. We would repeat nursery rhymes as Mom read them to us from my big Mother Goose Rhymes book with a large picture of a golden goose on the hard cover and a red trimming around the edge. I loved to listen to animal stories, too; that is, if they had "happily ever after" endings. I remember crying and feeling sad after watching the show "Bambi" at school. Ever since then, I cringed when I heard the word hunter. Besides reading and listening to stories, my sister and

I played house. We pretended to be grownups, dressing up in some of Mom's old dresses and hats, and holding our favourite dolls while we politely sipped imaginary cups of tea at the little, wooden table in the playhouse that Dad made for us. We cuddled our dolls and rocked them back and forth as we cooed and sang to them. Even though I had a newer doll, it was Baby Lovems, the tattered old doll with one arm hanging loosely and stuffing falling out of her ragged, cloth body, that I loved most of all. Being a child who on some days was a grownup was fun.

Chapter Three

I was so proud of my little sister. One day Mom and I took Lin to school. I remember my grade one teacher, Miss Curry, with a big smile on her face as she held my little sister on her lap. I also recall that my mother was the first one to show up in my grade three class on Parents' Day. She got to sit on the only adult chair in the room.

One winter we had a Talent Day in which each pupil was to participate. At home, Mom and I practised the song "White Christmas" for days. Finally, the special day came. Miss Huggins chose me to read the names of each pupil when it was his or her turn to perform. I conveniently skipped over my name when it was my turn to sing the song I'd practised for hours with Mom. I was always shy when it came to speaking or performing in front of a crowd. Each Christmas Season when I hear the music of this familiar popular song, there is always a small regret that I hadn't stood before the class on Talent Day to sing "White Christmas".

Mom was not only a good cook but she was also skilled when it came to sewing. I remember the pretty, red skirt with straps that she made for me. It had frills around the bottom. Placed on the front, right side was a little, white-laced doily with a tiny, black, velvet bow on top of it. I felt so proud wearing my new, red skirt to school. Dressed in it, together with having ringlets in my long, black hair, made it a very special day for me.

We had a family album which contained an assortment of photographs of the family, members of the family, friends, and special occasions. I remember looking through the album and seeing pictures of myself from the time I was about nine months old. Among them was a picture of Mom sitting on the front lawn with me on her lap, a picture of me smiling as I sat in my wooden high chair in the backyard, and one of my favourites when I was preschool age, sitting on a pony with dapple chocolate spots. I was wearing a straw hat, with a smug look on my face. A photographer had come along our street, offering to take our pictures for a very reasonable price. Mine was taken at the end of our block under a shady tree. And then there were all the school class pictures which were added to the photo album each year. I enjoyed looking back at how I had grown and changed each year. I always took a second look at myself sitting on the cute pony and my grade three picture in which I wore my pretty, red skirt, with its straps and frilly bottom, with my hair done in pretty, little ringlets.

Chapter Four

Sir Arnold Johnston was the elementary school I attended for almost six years. It was only two blocks from my house, so I usually took a shortcut down the lane. I remember one of the boys named Billy, a casual friend of my brothers who lived across the lane a few houses down, teasing me and not wanting to let me pass him. He was one of the show-off boys who sometimes played with other boys on my block. I scowled, screwed up my nose and stuck out my tongue, then gave him a quick jab before running away as fast as I could. Behind me I heard loud snickering. Now I understood why BB, a nickname he had, wasn't accepted as one of the regular group on my street. I think BB stood for Big Billy, but to me it was Bully Billy. This is one time I told Mom about the incident. After Billy received a tongue lashing from her and my brother, I never had any more trouble. As a matter of fact, BB was snubbed by the boys when they heard of the lane incident. He finally got the picture when he was always the last one to be chosen for a team game and when he wasn't invited to John's last birthday party. Feeling sorry for him, I invited him to our Hallowe'en party. There was a noticeable change in his attitude after that. We even became good friends.

I always managed to get to school before the bell rang. Each week the older students took turns being a bell monitor. Their duty was to stand at the top of the outside stairs and swing the hand bell back and forth each day before and after school as well as at recess and lunchtime. During our breaks I would play double dutch or hopscotch. Sometimes at lunch time I would join in a baseball game for fun. I usually ran home for lunch but the odd time I'd purchase a small, coloured, plastic tag for soup or a hot lunch like macaroni and cheese or shepherd's pie. I found the bought lunch a real treat.

The only year I wasn't eager to go to Sir John Arnold School was when the school day was divided into two shifts due to overcrowding. I was one of the unlucky pupils who managed to be in the early shift, which began at eight o'clock. The afternoon shift began at twelve o'clock. I suppose the advantage was that I arrived home early when some of my schoolmates were still busy at school. Fortunately, the administration must have found a solution to the problem, because within three months we were back to our usual routine.

If there were two favourite days of the week I looked forward to, I would choose Wednesday and Friday. On Wednesdays the nurse would make her rounds to each classroom with a bottle of brown pills called thyroid pills. These pills didn't taste at all like the bitter, cod liver oil pills that I took at home. They had a smooth, chocolaty taste like vico. I really liked Fridays. First of all, it was the day before the weekend, and secondly, it was hot lunch day. The other four days of the school week I went home for lunch. On Fridays I ate lunch in the cafeteria. We purchased advance tickets for soup or a wholesome meal like macaroni and cheese or shepherd's pie. Soup cost three cents and the hot lunch was five cents. As the volunteer lunch workers came to our tables with trays of the hot, savoury-smelling food, we'd hold up our tags waving our arms as we called out, "Soup! Soup!" or "Hot lunch! Hot lunch!" To finish off our meal we each received a slice of fruit. I thought Friday was a great day.

One of my favourite subjects was spelling. We'd have two teams and each person on a team would take turns spelling a word. After a specific amount of time, the team with most players left was the winning team. I remember the one and probably only time my grade five teacher, Mr. Adams, who I thought was young and handsome, told me I ranked first in his class. When I told Mom and Dad the happy news at suppertime, they smiled and Dad jokingly said, "I guess that means you were the rankest in the class." I chuckled, too, sort of guessing what rankest meant.

Although PE was a time we could let off some of our energy, I didn't look forward to the exercise when you had to lie flat on your back and then turn to your side. I had pretty big bony hips for the rest of my frame and the grimace on my face showed that lying on a hip was no fun. I had pictures in my head of my hips being black and blue. It was always a relief when we had a game of volleyball even though the inner part of my hand usually stung after serving the ball. All in all, I still thought PE could be a fun time and tried hard to be a good sport.

Although according to me I was a well-behaved pupil, there was the after-school incident when a few of my friends and I were called into the principal's office for grabbing hands, spreading out, and running down the middle of the road. The next day we were called into the principal's office where we were admonished for our foolish behaviour. After a lecture on safety with Mr. Hend's hand placed on the top of my head, that was the end of our escapades.

Being Chinese never made me feel different from others at home, at school, or anywhere I went. I was just part of the Charles Street group in my white neighbourhood. Like most typical youngsters, I kept busy with schoolwork, activities, and playing with my sisters and neighbourhood friends. When I was in grade three, I began taking piano lessons. There was a piano in the house since Mom played. I didn't mind practising and enjoyed the pieces in the Royal Conservatory books. I always seemed to be busy with schoolwork and all kinds of activities.

After doing our homework we sometimes spent rainy days playing all sorts of games. Board games like Monopoly or Clue, card games like fish or snap, and checkers/Chinese checkers were regulars. Pick-up sticks and jacks were lots of fun, too. One day Dad surprised us by making a Crokinole board. It was a smooth, round, two-toned, brown, wooden board with inserted pegs in its shiny surface, a round hole in the middle, and a trough around the edge. The aim of the game was to flick discs into the centre hole of the round board or into higher-value fields to gain the most points. It was fun and exciting as the opposing players tried to hit one another's discs to one of the lower value fields or completely off the board. The zones nearest the centre of the board were worth 15 points, decreasing to 5 points closest to the trough. Your little round discs were either black or beige depending which team you were on. Of course, everyone would hope to hit the bullseye which was the centre hole worth a whole twenty points. Whenever my team won, I would excitedly shout a loud "YEAH!" even with my sore stinging thumb.

On dry days the neighbourhood kids would gather and play tag, hide-and-go-seek, and red rover. Sometimes we would ride our bicycles or roller skate up and down the sidewalk. Like most kids my age, there were times when we'd have our little spats, but got over them as quickly as they had started. I don't remember my parents ever shouting or speaking harshly to us, but in a kind manner with firmness, explaining right from wrong. Something that was never tolerated in our house was using name calling, vulgar language, or swearing. Probably the nearest thing to cursing that I ever heard kids on my street say was "darn" or "heck". Occasionally a couple show-off boys from down the lane joined our group activities. They tried to act tough in front of the girls by using off-colour words. I would cringe, plug my ears, and try to ignore them. Tattling was a no-no. Billy, nicknamed BB short for Big Billy due to his size, would get on my nerves at times with his teasing. I'd be playing one, two, three a lerry with my lacrosse ball, when suddenly it would bounce up and manage to be grabbed by BB. Or I'd be skipping rope when a hand from behind tugged on it. BB was good at spoiling my fun. He could be a real pain. Luckily Danny would sometimes come to my rescue . . . good, old Danny. He might have been much smaller than BB, but he was a good friend. I was the friend in need and he was a friend indeed.

I was no angel, either. If I wanted to, I could be stubborn, silent, or pout. If I really disliked something one of my so-called friends had done or said to irk me, I would try to get even with them by making a face at them, say something nasty with the hopes of hurting their feelings, and end with a na-a, na-a, ne na-a na-a in a singing up-down tone. By the next day, the whole episode had been forgotten and we were back to our usual playing.

During the summer with its hot days, all the kids on my block were anxious to hear the familiar tune of the roaming ice cream truck. It didn't take long before a throng of us would be standing at the open window of the truck holding up our dimes for an ice cream treat. My favourite was a vanilla Dixie cup. I'd quickly pull up the tiny tab on the lid as I yearned to dig into my cold, yummy ice cream with a small, oval-shaped, wooden spoon. Within minutes the novelties were gone and all the satisfied kids were back playing. In our house we didn't have to wait until the summer time to have our ice cream. As a matter of fact, we could have it anytime during the year. Our milkman delivered a bottle of fresh milk to our door daily. At the very top of the milk was a layer of cream. Mom would use it to make ice cream. The cream was mixed with ice cubes and a little sugar, and then set in the fridge freezer in an ice cube tray until it was completely frozen. Mom's delicious homemade ice cream had a different texture and flavour from that which we got from the ice cream truck, but it was just as good if not better—M-M-M.

Some days when we played outdoors, I

would practise standing on my head, doing somersaults, cartwheels, backbends and handstands. I was determined to learn to walk on my hands. I never did master that or do the proper splits. I would always be an inch from the ground, attempting to do the splits. The only time they appeared perfect was when I practised them on my bed, which had a fluffy thick comforter on top of it.

The odd time one of my neighbour friends would invite me for a sleepover or I'd reciprocate and have them stay at my house overnight. I always felt most comfortable in my own double bed at home which I shared with my little sister. It was fun staying at a friend's for a change, but there was nothing like returning the next day to sleep in my own bed in my own home. I was like a boomerang, always coming back to where I'd started.

I had become good friends with Jeanie, a grade four classmate. We'd each visited one another's house and had met the parents previously. Jeanie lived several blocks away from me. One day to my surprise I was asked to sleep over at her house. This was a new experience for me. When I climbed into her narrow, wooden bed beside her, it collapsed. Jeanie's father managed to fix the homemade bed temporarily while two stunned youngsters lay laughing boisterously, chatting, and giggling for the remainder of the night. Although we still continued playing at each other's house after school, I don't recall ever being asked to sleep over again.

The farthest I'd been away from my home and parents was the time Daddy Chen made a trip to one of his restaurants in a small town called Toursville which was hidden away in the Kootenays. Although I'd heard that it was well known for its winter skiing, I would be going for a week during the summer. I would stay with a family whom my natural father had met when he'd travelled there on other occasions to check his business. I suppose this was one way to become a little more acquainted with Daddy Chen.

Chapter Five

When we first arrived in Toursville, I was driven to the Beacon's house which was a large, gray house with a brown picket fence surrounding it. Four wide steps led to the long veranda where a bright, newly painted bench sat. A smiling mother with three daughters came down the stairs to greet us and carry my small suitcase into the house. I was taken upstairs where I spotted twin beds and a large bed which I thought I'd have all to myself. At home I was used to sleeping with my younger sister in a double bed. I later found out that I would be squished between two of the girls in the what seemed not-so-large bed.

Daddy Chen was anxious to get to the restaurant so he and I drove to the Jade Restaurant which was about a twenty-minute drive to town. Along the way we passed a large green golf course with avid golfers swinging their clubs and some boaters peacefully relaxing as their small boat glided around the small lake. We passed some young people on dirty mountain bikes as they pedalled by, smiling and waving their hands at us. This seemed like such a friendly town.

Daddy Chen seemed to know his way around. He parked the car on the main street. As we walked up the hilly sidewalk, people smiled and nodded. A couple people thought Daddy Chen looked familiar and stopped to say a few welcome back words to him and he proudly introduced his daughter to them. One old gentleman mentioned that we had to be sure to see the beautiful alpine wildflowers on the other side of town which were in full bloom.

As I stopped halfway up the hill and gazed about, the view of the stunning mountains surrounding this tiny tucked away town took my breath away. It was an incredible sight that I couldn't have imagined.

Suddenly I felt a nudge on my arm as Daddy Chen led me forward to our destination. Finally, we stopped at a large sign that read Jade Restaurant. This was Daddy Chen's restaurant. It was packed with the regular lunch crowd that had hearty appetites for Chinese food. Since no other restaurants served Chinese food, the line ups were usually long during lunch and dinner hours. I was led away from the crowd to a booth in the far corner where a waiter in a Chinese jacket served me a scrumptious meal: a bowl of egg drop soup with peas, chicken fried rice, chicken chow mein, and a mixture of green vegetables. Daddy Chen joined me, but even then I knew we wouldn't be able to finish this enormous meal, but the waiter smiled and remarked, "You can take the rest home with you." I sipped the remainder of my Chinese tea, and Daddy Chen and I walked hand in hand out of the restaurant with my container full of leftover food. This was probably the first time I felt the man beside me was not a stranger.

The ride home was more relaxed and, unlike the long distance of silence heading to Toursville, the time returning to Vancouver seemed much shorter. The journey to Toursville had helped to melt some of the ice between my biological father and me. But all the same I was relieved and overjoyed to see Mom and Dad who were waiting with open arms. l was back home again—home sweet home. It doesn't matter how far a boomerang is thrown, it will always come back.

Chapter Six

Across the street from my home lived a Scottish widower. The last time we visited Mr. Walker we brought him some Valentine's cookies which Mom, my sister, and I had fun decorating and baking for our school party. We would spot him sitting on the front stairs of his big gray-and-white house enjoying the sun and fresh air. That was our cue to scurry across the street and sit with Mr. Walker as he would tell us all kinds of stories using his brogue. We could listen to him for hours as he sang Scottish songs with his familiar burr. After he finished his repertoire, his hand would go into his pocket and magically out would pop the most delicious, sweet, beige, Sottish lifesavers that made our mouths water as we sucked on them.

Mr. Walker had an apple tree in his backyard. When the apples were ripe, we would wait eagerly at the side of his house where there was a fence, knowing that transparent apples would soon roll out for us to grab. After thanking Mr. Walker we would hurry home with our arms full of apples, which Mom made into delicious apple pies for us that day. We'd be sure that

Mr. Walker would get a big piece of Mom's scrumptious apple pie. What a fun day we had spent with Mr. Walker who was a very, very special, grand old neighbour. I think he enjoyed our company, too.

Watching Mr. Walker take bites of the special Valentine's Day cookies that we helped make reminded me of our last Valentine's Day party at school. A box was decorated by a group of us with pink and orange crepe paper. About two weeks before Valentine's Day, during art period, each student was given a piece of shiny, manila tag paper plus pieces of coloured paper from the scrap box. There was enough paper for each student to make at least two or three valentines which were dropped in the slot at the top of the Valentine's box. We had made a list of catchy words and phrases that could be written on the cards if we were stuck. Besides these valentines some students brought more valentines from Valentine's books that their parents had purchased. My family shared a Valentine's book which had over a hundred valentines of different shapes and words on them. Of course, there was always a special valentine for my teacher, and I always made sure to give a valentine to every girl and boy in my class. I even chose one for BB.

On Valentine's Day, the cards in the decorated box were given out. You could tell which pupils were the most popular by the number of valentines they received. I'm glad that I gave one to BB because you could tell from the number of valentines in his hand that he definitely wasn't the most popular boy in the classroom. As the kids in the room roamed around freely, there were lots of chuckles, ahs, and words of thanks. I loved all my cards with their fun pictures and messages. One valentine was a large cookie with red-and-white frosting. On it were the words "You are a real sweet cookie." On the back of it was written "your friend, Diane". Another was a picture of a clown with tears streaming down his cheeks. The message read "I'm so sad when you're not around." That card was from Danny. I guessed right away who the next valentine was from even before reading her name on the back. There was a picture of two girls kneading dough for bread. The message said "A friend in need is a friend indeed." On the back was "Love, from your friend, Aila". She was a good friend indeed. After looking at each card, I smiled or laughed. The last heart-shaped card had a picture of a boy giving a girl a small bouquet of flowers with a bee sitting on it. The message read "Roses are red, violets are blue, honey is sweet and so are you." When I turned the valentine over, there was another little poem but no signature. I read the little poem on the back.

From a frend who lives along the lane (friend)

Who sometimes can be a bit of a pane. (pain)
A frend (friend)
It didn't take me long to figure out who the

mysterious sender was. There were three kids in my class who live down the lane from me. But there was only one person I could think of who was a lousy speller, was terrible when it came to homonyms, and was worse at handwriting. BB was one of the two pupils in the classroom with the most illegible writing; I was the other one. Even practising the MacLean's cursive method of writing didn't help either of us. One good thing was that I was able to read anything a person wrote. Whenever my classmates couldn't decipher someone's message, I was the one to whom they came. When Chris came to me with his message from BB, that was the final confirmation of my mysterious valentine. I have to admit in spite of all past annoying tricks played on me by this prankster, my heart melted at his kind gesture. As I described my exciting day at school to my parents and showed them my bundle of cards, we gazed at the special one on the very top, the mysterious valentine that made the biggest impression on me that day with its sweet message from "you know who".

Aila was a special girlfriend who lived down the street from Mr. Walker. She was a blonde-haired girl, the same age as I was but a little taller and slightly plumper. Aila lived with an older sister since her parents had both died. My friend spent a lot of time at my house and would often join us at meal time. Weekends were often spent riding our bicycles or roller skating. We would hurry up to the next street which had a fairly steep hill, skate to the top, and come whizzing down, sometimes stopping ourselves at the bottom on our bottoms. We spent a lot of time at each other's house—singing, dancing, listening to music, chatting, and laughing.

One afternoon I was invited to have dinner at Aila's. Her sister, Meda, was always jovial and met me with fervour. She taught us a few fast dance steps and catchy, new piano tunes like chopsticks, which we pounded away as she disappeared into the kitchen with a pained look on her face. Then she called, "Dinner is served. Come and get it!" Meda made a humongous pot of Italian spaghetti accompanied by an unusual salad. Aila was used to her sister's salad concoctions. I was used to a simple lettuce salad with celery, onions, and tomatoes. When the dandelion salad was served, I politely said, "No thank you. I'll never finish this mountain of spaghetti", as I passed it to Aila. Since Aila didn't have any strange effects after dinner, I decided the next time I was offered Meda's salad, I'd graciously accept.

After helping clean up, since Hallowe'en was only a few days away, Aila and I decided we'd tell scary stories with the intention of frightening each other out of our boots. As kids we sometimes let our imaginations run wild. I got to go first, telling about my spooky experience using a low, trembling, haunting voice that made my friend shudder. In my house there was a long, dark, creepy closet where we hung our clothes between the two upstairs bedrooms. I would sometimes keep my eyes glued on that eerie closet, where I thought a ravenous monster might be lurking. I stared at the closet expecting the creature to jump out and pounce on me at any moment. Before I knew it, my blurry, tired eyes would close and I'd fall fast asleep.

Then Aila would try to freak me out with a spine-thrilling story involving slithering snakes and creepy spiders. She knew I was terrified of those slimy snakes, ever since Shelley had chased me with one, and another time one of those terrible, rough boys had run after me with a wiggly, legless reptile. I had a phobia to arachnids from the night I felt something tickling my foot. My giggling turned to a shriek when I pulled back the covers to find a large black spider on my foot. Now it was time to get even with Aila.

I then tried to top my friend's frightening story by telling her how one moonlit night I sensed a strange shadowy figure in my room, hovering overhead. Out of the corner of one eye, I could see this creepy, menacing shape with two horns emerging from its head and a long, bulky, dragon-like tail evolving from its enormous, hairy body move about, sometimes lingering on a bedroom wall or the ceiling. Holding my breath, I gingerly turned to one side, pulling the comforter over my ear. When I finally had the nerve to turn my head, peeking out from the protective comforter, I was relieved to spy Rosco, my fluffy, black-and-white cat, moving back and forth on my bedroom window sill, finally settling down in a lying position as he stared at the round, yellow moon against the pitch-black sky. Did I ever let out a huge sigh of relief that time! By the time we'd finished our storytelling, we were both so scared that we called Aila's older sister, who calmed both of us down and joined us for the rest of the evening. She had been in the kitchen, listening with a grin to our eerie stories.

Telling our tales at Aila's house after supper probably wasn't the best time, especially if the sun had gone down and it was getting darker by the minute. But my friend assured me that we were telling our chilling tales all in fun. All the same, when it was time to return home from her house, Aila would always watch me cross the street and run like lightning past the few bushes on our street in case the boogey man popped out. After that, we decided to change our stories drastically. Using our imaginations to describe pleasant or humorous experiences suddenly sounded much more appealing.

We always looked forward to summertime weekends when my family and two families across the lane went to White Rock for the day. Swimming, followed by a picnic meal, satisfied our appetites and quenched our thirst. Each summer holiday, Mom, my sisters, my girlfriend, and I would spend a week at White Rock using the trailer that Dad built. Wading in the warm pools, being careful not to step on little crabs for fear of having our feet pinched, running across the sandbars, and swimming in the ocean were fun times.

Chapter Seven

Our summer holidays seemed to go by so quickly. We knew that our days of leisure would soon be over when it was PNE time, a special event for us. We would be among the eager crowds lining Hastings Street where the PNE parade would travel its route with a variety of floats, marching bands, drum majorettes, jugglers, and comical clowns with balloons before our mesmerized eyes. Eventually the magical parade would come to a stop at the PNE grounds, where anxious people would flock to be the first ones through the gates.

Though we were anxious to attend the PNE, we would always wait until Children's Day when admission was free for us. Also, we knew if we shopped at Buy Me's Market on the last day of August, they'd be giving out free ride tickets to the first hundred customers of the day. That is one morning we all got up extra early. As usual, they handed out two tickets to each girl or boy under fourteen years old. Since we were regular customers at the store, the clerk who recognized us gave each of us an extra ticket. We could hardly wait until Children's

Day when we'd be sure to use up all the tickets.

Aila's older sister accompanied us to the PNE on Children's Day. Because it would have been too long of a day and the rides would have been too hard on her, Lin didn't come along. But we had planned two special events for her to attend within the next two weeks which she would find just as much fun; one was a circus and the other a petting zoo.

The PNE was about twelve blocks from our house, but we were used to walking that distance. Knowing where we were heading was all we cared about. The grounds were really crowded with kids that day, which was to be expected. The aroma of the popcorn, fries, and meat filled the air, but we were more interested in using our tickets on the rides and playing games.

My favourite ride was the merry-go-round, which was pretty tame in comparison to some of the others. I chose a shiny, black pony, which I held onto for dear life as it moved up and down to the fun fair music. Then Aila and I went on a more daring ride, the Ferris wheel, which I didn't mind until we rose to the top. I had warned Aila not to rock the seat as I clenched the bar. She was as scared as I was, so we both gave a sigh of relief when the wheel brought us back to the bottom. Although my legs felt like jelly, we decided to use our third ticket on the octopus ride. It looked like a huge monster with eight strong, steel legs that had carriages that would hold two to four persons in them. Four of us crammed ourselves into a carriage. We knew this would be a fast-moving ride but decided to be daredevils anyway. We climbed into our carriage, strapped our seatbelts tightly, and pulled the thick, silver bar towards us to lock us in. The octopus started off slowly but gathered more speed by the second. The next thing we knew was a swift turn every so often, which made my head spin. Everybody was yelling and screaming. Just as I thought I'd had enough, the octopus slowed down and finally came to a halt. Both Aila and I felt a little light-headed and agreed this was enough rides for the day. Meda, who was usually a few steps behind us but always keeping an eye on us, decided it was time to sit down on a bench and watch some of the outdoor stage performances. My favourite performance was the Tahitian dancers. It was amazing how they could wiggle their hips to the rapid, beating drums while the rest of their body didn't move at all.

After we rested up, our stomachs told us they needed replenishing, so we stopped for a hot dog and drink and finished off with some cotton candy. It wasn't really made of cotton but had a lot of sugar in it, which gave us energy to rush down to the game section. We always stopped at the dart game even though I never did manage to throw the dart into the middle; it was fun to try anyway. My favourite game was the one in which you got to roll a ping pong ball onto a spinning board which had four different colours around the board: red, blue, yellow, and green. The worker would press a button, which turned the round board, and you had four chances to roll the ball into certain matching colours. If you had two of a matching colour, you would win a small prize; if you had two of two matching colours, you would win a more expensive prize; if you had three of one colour, you would win an even more expensive prize, and so on. I almost always came home with a prize. Usually it was a glass or a fruit bowl, but never a large stuffed animal like I saw some kids carrying, which they won at other games, like the dart game. Just the same, I could look in Mom's cabinet and proudly say, "I won that at the PNE."

When I returned home, I was adamant on learning to move my hips rapidly without moving the upper part of my body, just like those beautiful Tahitian dancers. Unfortunately, it was easier said than done. After attempting to do this dance for several days, there was no improvement at all. When I looked at myself in the mirror and saw nothing but a bowl of jiggling jelly, I decided to give up. This exotic dance was not for me.

The following Saturday, my family went to the large recreational centre which held a Kiwanis Club Circus. It's always fun and thrilling to watch the many acts. I could see by the sparkle in Lin's wide eyes and the expression on her face that she was having a good time.

The ringmaster, with his red jacket and black pants, introduced each performance. First came a beautiful lady with a fancy, satin, pink jumpsuit trimmed in colourful sequins standing on a white stallion decorated with a matching pink, feathery collar and saddle. The lady stood on the horse, lifted one leg, and then leapt in the air, doing a backwards somersault, repeating this trick and various others as the majestic horse trotted or galloped around the ring. Then came the aerialists. The tight rope walker moved cautiously across the wire high in the air, and the daring trapeze artists leapt through the air, flying to moving bars on the other side. With each of these daring acrobatic acts would come sounds of amazement or fear from the open-mouthed audience, whispering or shouting expressions as they sat in the bleachers in awe, finally standing as they clapped and roared approval at the incredible feats of these performers. Although I would close my eyes and hold my breath, for fear of what might happen, knowing there was a safety net below set my mind at ease . . . when I remembered it was there.

I think we all relaxed when the ringmaster introduced the following act. I laughed so hard at the antics of the clowns. The clown on stilts was being chased by juggling clown. The big balloon rear end on another clown was popped by an apple-nosed clown zooming by on a unicycle. Every direction one looked was a clown with his hilarious antics. When a red-headed fat clown in a yellow polka dot jumpsuit with his hair sticking in the air and a painted face skipped up to us, we laughed until he looked as if he was going to throw a pail of water at us. We quickly ducked and were ready to be splashed, but to our surprise we were covered with popcorn, balloons, wrapped candies, and tickets for free sodas. Now that was a surprise, and it really made the afternoon at the circus special. We not only spent the next few days raving about the event, but even months later something would always pop up that brought back fond memories of a very, very special day at the circus.

The following Sunday was a perfect day to take Lin on the second event we had planned for her. First, we would go to church. Usually Sunday mornings our family would attend our church a few blocks away. The kids went to Sunday School and Aila and I joined the children's choir. Mom often played the organ for church services, and the children's choir sometimes sang a song during the service. The organist and the choir sat in the balcony, which was a good thing. My friend and I would sometimes get the giggles, especially when we heard one of the girls singing off key. We would gain our composure when Mom turned her head to see what the commotion was about.

In our church, the children took confirmation

lessons when they were twelve or thirteen years old. Fortunately, Aila wasn't there to distract me. We were taught many things, one of them being the Ten Commandments. We also learned about a God who loves us and to reflect this by showing love through our words and actions in our daily lives. Learning about God's love was one thing; reflecting it was another, especially in the next year or two.

Mom and Dad decided in the afternoon we would take a drive to a small community about two hours away. At the end of summer nearby farms would bring their farm animals to the small town of Anderby. Before the beginning of a new school year, parents would bring their children to the little zoo, where they could learn about the animals and have a chance to pet and feed them. Although we had a soft, cuddly pet rabbit before, we had never petted or fed a sheep, goat, or pig so this was an experience for us. It was a coincidence that my parents' friend, Mr. Wilson, who owned a farm nearby, happened to be at the zoo at the same time we were there. He invited us to see some of his other farm animals that afternoon.

What an amazing time we had! There were chickens, pigs, lambs, kids, and two ponies. I had sat on a dappled pony when I had my picture taken, but I had never actually ridden on a pony before. Lin was first to ride on one of the ponies. Mr. Wilson helped her onto a black-and-white pony named Spotty. He was a cute fellow with big, brown eyes, and moved his head gently as I petted his muzzle. Lin's face lit up as Mr. Wilson's son Tommy led Spotty along a path on the farm made especially for the ponies to take children on short rides. As Lin was lifted down from Spotty, she thanked Tommy and Spotty for the delightful ride. It had been her first time on a pony and she could hardly wait to tell everyone of her experience. Then it was my turn. Tommy helped me onto the saddle on Spotty's back. I felt as if I were on top of the world. Roy Rogers and Hop-A-Long Cassidy, here I come. Then one of Mr. Wilson's helpers took the reins and led me around the yard. One by one, we all had a turn on Spotty. It was a wonderful afternoon. When it was time to leave, we all rushed up to Mr. Wilson, thanking him for this incredible farm experience. And then rushing up to Spotty, he received a big hug from each of us with a wide grin and "thank you, Spotty!" to which he replied with a nod and whinny. I think this was a fun day for Spotty, too.

Chapter Eight

Like all children, I love surprises and special occasions. I remember the tooth fairy secretly coming whenever I lost a tooth. In the morning I would wake up, look under my pillow, and find a coin. I recall the day I came home from the dentist's office missing a few teeth. That was one of the days when I sat in the chair at the dentist's having a few teeth extracted and wishing instead I was lined up with all the other excited kids eager to watch a show in the theatre which I could see across the street where my eyes were focused. I think Mom felt so sorry for me having four teeth removed that the following morning I not only wakened to a coin under my pillow, but with it was a bottle of pink hand lotion. Maybe removing a few teeth was worth it after all.

Hallowe'en was always a day we looked forward to with the fun and excitement beginning at school with a jack–o'-lantern contest, a masquerade parade, and a Hallowe'en party filled with fun games and yummy treats. After a light supper we would eagerly dress up in our costumes again, carrying the pillowcases we hoped to fill with treats, as a group of us scampered up and down the streets trick-or-treating. Our pillowcases were stuffed with popcorn balls, candy apples, chocolate bars, liquorice sticks, and different-coloured candies. We always ended out our Hallowe'en by watching the fireworks display put on by my married sister's husband. Elsie and Jeffrey would come over every Hallowe'en evening to put on a big show for the kids on my street. We weren't allowed to touch any of the fireworks except the sparklers, which each of us were permitted to hold. Our eyes and ears were opened to the loud sound, high-pitched whistles, and sprays of sparks as each of the firework items spun rapidly or shot off sprays of coloured sparks into the sky lit up by the astonishing display. Before settling down for an unforgettable evening, I would sort out my treats and put them in a large bowl. Each day I would take out a treat, making sure to leave the ones I liked the very best until last. As I nibbled on the treats, etched in my mind was the previous fantastic night when we strutted along the dark, bewitching route, finally to be lit up by the brilliant sparks of light on our street.

December seemed to be such a busy month for us. Besides realizing that the Christmas season would soon be upon us, Dad and I would be celebrating our birthdays at the beginning of the month. It just so happened that they were on the same day. It was fun and exciting giving and receiving presents. Mom and all of us pooled our money and gave Dad a hammer, nails, and garden gloves. I received a little bracelet, a book on pets, and a pair of figure skates. I couldn't believe my eyes. I had always rented ice skates and now I had my very own. Someday I was going to be the second Barbara Ann Scott. After the opening of gifts, Mom came out with a beautiful homemade birthday cake with flowers on top that my sisters had helped to decorate. On it were the birthday wishes "Happy birthday, Dad and Carly". Before we blew out the candles, Dad and I made our wishes. Usually my wishes were silly. One time I wished that I could stand on my hands for five minutes. Another time I wished that I had a watch like Patty, the richest girl I know. There was one time I actually wished for someone else, my little sister. I really wished that she would have a healthy heart to match her good heart. On this birthday I couldn't think of anything else that I wanted or hoped. I had such a wonderful loving family. We were all together. We would soon be celebrating a time of joy, peace, and love. What else could I wish for?

Preparing for and celebrating the Christmas Season was one of the highlights of the year. I remember walking down Hastings Street with Mom and going shopping in all the stores, looking for just the right present for everyone. For Mom and Dad I chose a lovely round, glass platter with three compartments in the middle for appetizers, surrounded by an etched, elegantly floral-designed area for desserts. The lovely dish was embossed with a simple-yet-ornate, thin, gold trimming. For my siblings I picked out little, silver, storybook boxes which contained an assortment of different-flavoured lifesavers. Each of us took a few pennies from our allowance with a little extra money from Mom to buy a small gift for a needy child. Most of the presents were purchased at Woolworth's, a nickel and dime store. I could hardly wait to sneak the hidden presents under the Christmas tree.

During the Christmas Season our church would collect donations of food and money, which would go towards hampers and gifts for individuals or families to help brighten their Christmas a little. We were among the carolers who spent an evening singing favourite carols at their doors and presenting them with a gift before singing the last song "We Wish You a Merry Christmas". We had a warm feeling in our hearts when our Christmas wish of peace, joy, and love along with a small gift was accepted with a smile, thank you, and the tears in their eyes.

I think all children hope for snow during the winter season, especially for Christmas. One year we had an exceptionally snowy winter to our delight. All the children on the block would have a snowman contest to see who could build the most original snowman of all.

We'd laugh and shout as each snowman took on its own unique shape. We'd either hum or sing "Frosty the Snowman" and sometimes the girls would shout above the boys, "Mrs. Frosty the Snowlady". There would inevitably be a snowball fight between the boys and girls. By the time the day's event came to a close, with rosy cheeks and cold hands everyone was ready for a warm cup of cocoa and sweet cookies which the mothers had waiting for us. After removing our wet snowsuits and boots, we ran for the register which blew heavenly heat on our chilled bodies. OOOH! Did it ever feel good! Sipping hot cocoa and gobbling yummy cookies was a perfect ending for a glorious fun day.

Decorating the Christmas tree was an exciting family event. I remember the colourful lights, the pretty, glass tubes with bubbly, sparkling water, the variety of ornaments, and silver tinsel icicles that we put on the Christmas tree. At the very top of the tree was a silver-haired angel in a soft pink robe. The whole tree with the angel and all the lights brightened up the front room, helping to make the season a special time to celebrate.

On Christmas Eve, we went to church, sang Christmas carols, and performed the Nativity Story. When we came home, our faces lit up when we saw all the presents under the tree. It was a tradition in our house to open our gifts on Christmas Eve. Then, since we didn't have a fireplace, we'd hang our stockings on a fir bough. Though we didn't get much sleep that night, early Christmas morning we woke up wide-eyed to find our gift-laden stockings filled with all sorts of surprises. Among them were a Mandarin orange and a red-and-white striped candy cane. After emptying our stuffed stockings, we quickly put on our Sunday's best and with bright eyes and happy faces attended the Christmas Day Service. We spent the rest of the day admiring and showing off our presents, trying on our new mittens and socks, and playing new board games in a house filled with the savoury, mouth-watering aroma of a turkey cooking in the oven.

Chapter Nine

My biological father, who was known to us as Daddy Chen, would allow my sister and me to be foster children but would never allow us to be adopted. I suppose he had other future plans. Although we didn't see him very often because of his busy schedule with his two restaurants, there was a concerted effort always made for us to meet him at least two or three times a year at one of his restaurants. One of the restaurants was downtown, a couple blocks from the area where we'd sometimes do a little shopping. One day it was near lunchtime, so both Mom and I decided to visit Daddy Chen's restaurant and have a bite to eat.

The restaurant was called Loon's, more than likely because it was on Loon Street. In the middle of the room were small- and medium-sized tables covered with white, plastic cloths designed with black-and-white loons in a peaceful setting. Along one side of the room were booths with soft, red, comfortable seats. Daddy Chen was at the register near the front entrance. By the expression on his face, we could tell that he was surprised but happy to see us. After a few words of welcome and introducing us to a couple waiters, we were led to a table. A bowl of soup and club sandwich was all we wanted, but Daddy Chen insisted it was not enough and had the waiters bring us two more special dishes that the cooks had made. Of course, the meal was on the house.

By the time we were finished our large meal, every waiter in the restaurant had come over to say hello to their boss' daughter and her foster mother. Even the kitchen cooks wanted to meet me. Traipsing through the swinging doors, I found myself in the kitchen where I met the chef and cooks who were busily bustling back and forth as they attempted to shout above the clanging of the banging steel spoons against the sizzling oil and steaming water in the woks as they cooked the meals for the hungry, waiting customers. The clamour, laughing, high-pitched conversing, and cooking came to a sudden stop when the employer appeared with his unannounced daughter. The lively atmosphere resumed as the chef and each cook had a turn at saying a few words in Chinese and then in English. Most of the Chinese was gibberish to me, but I could tell by the looks on everyone's face that I was a welcome sight and wished much happiness. Each one took a minute to shake my hand and say a few words. I understood the words "good girl"; "pretty girl". All I could do was smile and say "do je, do je" (thank you, thank you) and "ho sik, ho sik" (good eat or good tasting), as I pointed to the food in the woks. Then back went the cooks to their large woks over flaming fire, filled with the savoury detectable aroma of Chinese cuisine, and I walked proudly out the swinging door. This had been an unforgettable day for everyone, especially for me.

Two weeks before Chinese New Year, the family was invited to Daddy Chen's other restaurant which served Chinese cuisine. Jun Yook was a large restaurant located in the heart of Chinatown. After climbing a few carpeted stairs, we were met by Daddy Chen at the front desk. He turned his head to beckon a waiter dressed smartly in a black Chinese jacket with gold trimming around the cuffs and bottom edge of the uniform. As he started to show my family to its table, I had to stop at the large aquarium filled with different species of fish swimming about. There must have been at least six different kinds of fish in the tank. I remember having a goldfish once but the poor thing didn't last long. We had also been at the Stanley Park Aquarium so I had seen lots of beautiful fish. There were so many that I didn't remember the names of most of them. We all stopped to admire these tiny creatures of the sea. Noticing our interest in the fish, Daddy Chen called one of the waiters named Jimmy who had an interest in fish since he had an aquarium at home. He'd been doing a fair amount of reading on the little creatures so he was the perfect person to enlighten us on the subject of aquarium fish.

I thought all orange fish were called goldfish but learned that swordtails and platies were also gold. Apparently, the swordtails and platies are similar in appearance and behaviour but the swordtails are a bit slimmer and sleeker. Jimmy also told us that some fish are more aggressive than others. Not all fish can be put in the same tank or a few might be mysteriously missing. It's important to know which fish belong together. Guppies, netras, and neons are small, colourful critters who get along together. They were swimming back and forth between the freshwater plants. Then Jimmy suggested a few books that he found interesting and helpful. Fish and aquariums seemed to be the main topic around the dinner table that night. I realized that we had a lot to learn if we ever decided to have another aquarium.

That evening I think we had an early Chinese New Year banquet dinner consisting of at least twelve courses, beginning with a soup and ending with a sweet one. I hardly had time to try one dish before another was set on our table. I was willing to try a little of everything. I can't remember what all I ate that night but everyone was filled to the hilt. Each time a waiter brought a new dish, he'd tell us what it was, how to pronounce it in Chinese, and explained the meaning of the word and the good wishes it would bring. For example, fish meant surplus and wealth; roasted pig meant peace; lobster meant endless money rolling in. Finally, our dessert was a sweet pudding and oranges. The dessert meant wishes of sweetness, and the fruit meant wishes of abundance and happiness.

Before leaving, we thanked Daddy Chen for the heavenly banquet and Jimmy for enlightening us on fish for freshwater aquariums. Our evening was like a magical dream. We'd had a meal fit for a royal family. I had heard the word VIP mentioned before. Now I knew what it meant and what it felt like to be one.

There would be special times of the year when Daddy Chen would visit us at home. He hardly seemed like the same person we visited at his restaurant where he was constantly on the move, talking to the waiters and cooks, smiling and seemingly joking at times, and making friendly conversation with his customers. As I took a closer look at him, I noticed that this serious-looking man was shorter than Dad but taller than Mom and a bit on the thin side. He had straight, black hair with a wisp of gray here and there, and wore gold-rimmed glasses that sat on his flat nose. He would inevitably be dressed up, usually wearing a gray, pinstripe suit. I figure he was about the same age as my parents. To me, he seemed rather proper, occasionally smiling, but never laughing. In comparison to some of the jovial relaxed grownups I've seen, Daddy Chen seemed rather uptight and poker faced. Whenever he visited us, as the clock ticked on in our friendly house, he became used to the more relaxed atmosphere, and by the expression on his face and less rigid body I could tell he gradually felt more at ease. Studying his face carefully, I could see the resemblance I bore to him, unlike that of my little sister who must have looked more like my biological mother with her fine, feminine features. Usually Daddy Chen would visit us once or twice a year. I didn't especially look forward to his visits. It always seemed a bit strange. Even though I'd spent a week with him when I went to Toursville, this man was still a bit of a stranger.

I remember him sitting politely at our dining room table for a Thanksgiving meal. As we ate our delicious turkey meal, combined with exciting chatter, when he had the opportunity, Daddy Chen occasionally joined in on the conversation, speaking a few words with his slightly Chinese accent. He even participated in the wishbone custom that we explained to him and demonstrated of two of us wishing on the same turkey bone and then snapping it in half. I yelled, "Yeah, I get my wish!" when I got the bigger half. Daddy Chen just chuckled. His next visit was around Christmastime. Mom and Dad always made him feel welcome on his short visits. I wasn't sure how I felt.

I do remember Daddy Chen bringing my sister and me woollen dresses. They were the complete opposite of frilly and fancy, being made of a red-and-black plaid material with a tailored look. Daddy Chen probably thought we would look very nice in them. I'm sure we smiled and thanked him for the presents. The only problem was that I hated anything woollen against my skin. Just thinking about it made me start scratching all over. I most likely only wore the woollen dress when Daddy Chen visited which would please him. We even had our pictures taken wearing the woollen dresses. Daddy Chen didn't realize this was my few hours of torture. You can bet that as soon as he was gone, so was the itchy dress for something more comfortable.

Mom and Dad decided that we should learn a bit of Chinese. They thought if I could say a few words in Chinese such as "how are you" or count to ten, this would not only surprise Daddy Chen the next time he visited but also make him extremely happy. There was a Chinese church a block over from our church, not far from our house, so on weekends Dad would give me a ride to the church, where the pastor gave free lessons to children. Whatever I learned, I would teach my little sister. I learned a few basic words and phrases. When Daddy Chen visited the next time, I greeted him with nay ho ma (How are you?) then I told him my new Chinese vocabulary—ba ba means father and ma ma means mother. I also learned to say mgoy (please) and do je (thank you) which amazed Daddy Chen. From the wide grin that appeared on his face and the words he repeated ho, ho, (very good), we could tell that he was extremely pleased.

Chapter Ten

Days, weeks, months, years passed, and before I knew it, I was already in grade five. I enjoyed school even though at times I had to study hard. My favourite subject was English, and for some unknown reason at the bottom of the list were math and science.

Life seemed to be normal as I carried on with the usual routine and activities. I was my happy self until things changed when I was halfway through grade six. For some reason, Mom and Dad seemed a bit more quiet and serious. I hadn't realized that there were events to come that were weighing heavily on their minds. I was soon to find out the reason.

After several years, my biological father, Daddy Chen, decided to remarry. Once this occurred, he wanted his two daughters to live with him and his new wife. This was a devastating blow to Mom, Dad, my sister, and me. Why would anyone want to take their children away from loving parents who had raised their children? To me, my real parents were my foster parents. They were the only mother and father we had known and wanted to know.

The case was brought before the court and to our dismay the other party won. I imagined myself stomping into the courtroom and blurting out my feelings before the judge. I asked him whether he had any children. How would he feel if they were taken away from him? Was it right for him to make this life-altering decision without listening to my side of the story? Had he heard of the many years that my sister and I had lived with the only real parents that we knew and wanted to know? This judge had no idea how we were being torn apart on the inside and eventually we would be torn apart on the outside. If only the judge had an ounce of compassion and deep down had considered how my sister and I felt, maybe the decision would have been different—maybe.

The Children's Aid Society became involved in the matter, and my sister and I were soon visiting a Social Worker on a regular basis. Mrs. M., an older, official-looking lady, was the social worker who handled our case. Maybe the procedure for children going through a traumatic experience involved talking with a social worker in order to ease the pain and emotional state they were in. Anyway, it was arranged for my sister and me to go to the CAS building with her. It was a drab, gray building containing several areas on different levels. The room my sister and I entered was on the second floor. Except for a couple of round tables surrounded by a few chairs, a bookcase with a variety of children's books, and a shelf with boxes of pencils, crayons, paper, paint brushes, and small containers of paint, it was fairly empty. I thought it was strange when we were given crayons or some kind of writing material to scribble, print, or draw on the wall. Why anyone would think of messing up a wall was beyond me. I suppose it was a type of therapy to help alleviate the frustrations that this whole situation placed upon us. Luckily Daddy Chen wasn't there. The way I felt at this point, some of the material might have been used on him.

Chapter Eleven

As days went by, it seemed as if we were visiting my soon-to-be stepmother and her relatives on a weekly basis. Maybe I was just imagining what was happening or didn't really believe or understand the situation. Being rather naive to the situation, I decided to cooperate. On Sunday afternoons, Daddy Chen and his female friend would pick my sister and me up and take us on an outing.

One Sunday we went to Stanley Park, a lovely park surrounded by colourful flowers and all kinds of trees which provided a cool shade on stifling, hot days. I recognized the maple and alder as well as the tall fir and hemlock trees which were in a book on B.C. trees which had been given to me for my birthday. In the centre of the park was Lost Lagoon, a little pond with ducks and swans swimming about. We strolled along the pathway surrounding the little lake. As we sauntered down the pathway, we spotted a mother raccoon with her little ones. Trying to show my knowledge of raccoons, I spouted off, "A group of baby raccoons is called a nursery or a gaze", to which everyone gave me a gazed look. The little critters were so cute, I wanted to pick one up and cuddle it in my arms, but we were taught to look at, not touch or feed, certain wild animals. We watched the little ones for a few minutes, and then continued our walk as we eyed the beauties of nature. We were famished in no time, so stopped for a small bite. Daddy Chen had brought a small cloth shopping bag containing a big white box and a smaller red box. In the larger box were Chinese buns with different fillings. My first bun had barbecued pork inside. The second one had minced black beans. After downing our buns and finishing a sweet dessert, we continued our short stroll. It had been an unexpected day—an interesting and exciting time to become more acquainted with two people with whom future days would soon be spent.

Two weeks later, Daddy Chen and his friend took us to a field where a sports game was being played. I had seen lots of baseball and soccer games. Dad had been a baseball coach when my brother played for on a little league. But this game was different from any I had seen before. It was called walking jiju. The players used a hollow ball which was about the size of tennis ball. It was usually made of a light wood which had been carved with beautiful patterns. The goal of jiju was to hit the ball with a stick, somewhat like a lacrosse stick, into the opposing team's net. I think it was a cross between hockey and polo.

The third time Daddy Chen phoned and wanted to take us out was enough for me. I decided to be obstinate and made up the excuse that I had a bad stomach ache. It wasn't a complete lie because the more I thought about spending another Sunday afternoon away from home with two almost strangers, the more I felt sick to my stomach.

The next time spent with Daddy Chen and his lady friend wasn't exciting or interesting. In fact, it was downright boring. Usually going to a movie is a treat, but the Chinese movie we watched that afternoon was anything but. Watching Chinese warriors fighting with swords and listening to a Chinese dialogue which I didn't understand wasn't my kind of movie entertainment. I covered my eyes for most of the gruesome scenes and plugged my ears when it got too noisy even though I didn't know what the characters were shouting. I just knew it wasn't good. I thought, "I'd much rather be watching a good old action western movie with one of my favourite cowboys like Gene Autry, Hop-A-Long Cassidy, or Roy Rogers with his horse Trigger."

I didn't really look forward to the weekends when we were being slowly introduced to a new culture. But rather than pour out my true feelings, I kept silent when I'd like to have shouted at my biological father. I'd like to have shouted on the rooftops, "I know what you're up to! Why do you want to take us away from the people and home we love?" On the other hand, Lin seemed to take everything in her stride. She seemed more relaxed than I was and tended to be more talkative and actually enjoyed some of the outings. I figured being two years younger made a difference in the way we saw things, felt, and acted.

Finally, the dreaded day came when my sister and I were taken away from Mom and Dad. Mom and Dad didn't want my sister and me to be more upset than we were. They wanted to make the transition as easy as possible for us. There were no outbursts, no shouting, no words, no outward tears. Inwardly there were broken hearts, quiet sobbing, prayers for what was to come, hope, and the question "Why is this happening to us? Please, Lord. Please don't let them take us away! Please, Lord!"

I don't remember who drove us to our new home. Perhaps I'd rather not remember that day. It might have been our social worker. All I knew was that I was not where I wanted to be and definitely not with whom I wanted to be. I was brought up to obey so I didn't argue with anyone. I just remained silent. I was the older sister who had the responsibility of looking out for my younger, fragile sister.

Chapter Twelve

The first while we lived in a large house near Chinatown while Daddy Chen and his new wife were busy fixing and painting a more permanent place where we would live. I remember the night my sister and I were alone in the first house. My sister fell asleep, but I felt uneasy as we lay in bed so I kept my eyes open. Time seemed to drag on as the minutes went by. Then I heard something or someone downstairs. The sound seemed to be getting louder. Hearing footsteps coming near the bedroom, I held my breath. I gave a big sigh of relief when Daddy Chen and my stepmother opened the door, holding ice cream cones. It was the first time I'd even attempted to make the effort to give a brief smile. It was as if my mouth was pulled like an elastic band and released with a sudden snap back to its original shape.

A month or two later we moved into the Keefer Street house. It was a large house with an empty room in front which had probably been a store at one time. This barren room came in handy later when we wanted to run off a little steam.

Those who know me can tell you when I felt like it, I could be silent and stubborn. These traits could come in handy given the right situation. At first, I used them quite often, but as time went on, I became a little more lax. One thing I was adamant about was never to call Daddy Chen and his wife Mommy and Daddy. Somehow I always avoided addressing them period. They must have gotten used to this because the subject was never raised. My little sister may have been petite but her heart was much bigger than mine. Unlike her older sister, she would show kindness through her words and actions. On days when I appeared mopey and grouchy, she would cheer me up. She was a good example for all of us. Perhaps that's why as my attitude slowly improved, there seemed to be more peace and harmony in the house.

As the five of us, including my half-brother whom we just met, sat around the oval table, things were quite different. Jimmy was only three years old and unlike me didn't seem to mind his new environment. Very few words were spoken as we politely ate our food. I might have politely answered with, "Yes please", or "No thank you", or nodded my head for yes or no. We mostly listened to the Chinese spoken. Sometimes simple English phrases with a Chinese accent were heard. My stepmother to whom I referred was given the name Soo. She was a middle-aged lady, taller and bigger boned than the average Chinese woman. Like most Chinese women her age, she dyed her short, permed hair black. Although the older Chinese expected respect from the youngsters, I found it strange that the women wanted to appear younger. But a fifty-year-old, gray-haired Chinese woman would stand out like a purple-and-green zebra among a herd of black-and-white zebras.

Soo was a very good cook. At mealtime we had rice with stirred Chinese vegetables and small pieces of meat. This type of meal was quite different from the potatoes, vegetables, and meat that we had at home like yummy potatoes, stew, roast, or chicken accompanied by a glass of milk. I have to admit Soo made delicious meals which I had never tasted before. The first thing we had to learn was how to use chopsticks. I soon learned the names of a few vegetables and meat in Chinese. One of my favourite dishes included lup cheong (Chinese sausages). We drank milk while Soo and Daddy Chen had tea at suppertime so I soon learned to say ngou ni and cha. I'm sure to a native speaking Chinese, I had a real Canadian English accent.

Shopping in Chinatown was a weekly chore for Soo. The crowded streets were always buzzing with people buying produce, meats, and dried goods for cooking. I turned my head when a butcher would take a fresh fish which I knew would soon meet its fate. The idea of buying chicken's feet or pig's feet didn't appeal to me although when Soo cooked them up for a meal, they were quite tasty. We passed a corner store, and I mean passed, after seeing chocolate covered beetles in a bottle considered as a treat. When a lady walking by with a plate of samples offered me one, I almost passed out.

I found the store with odds and ends in it to my liking. I was pleased with my purchase of a pretty, bright red fan decorated with flowers and birds. I bought one with a different decoration on it for my sister. Just before we were about to leave, Soo wanted to stop at an herbal medicine store. I didn't stay in there long because of its pungent smell which seemed to penetrate my taste buds. It reminded me of the cod liver oil pill that Mom had us take on a daily basis. Why is it that medicine that is supposed to help children from being sick makes them feel sick when they take it? I was glad to leave the store and ready to return home . . . I mean to what was called our home. I had heard everyone speaking a language that I didn't understand so Soo would be the interpreter. When a clerk spoke to me and I looked at him with a puzzled look, I think he thought I was from another planet, especially when I attempted to answer him in Chinese and then English. It was much safer to smile and say nothing. I could get into trouble by saying what I thought was correct with the incorrect intonation. For example, I heard that using the word "doh see" could mean toast or mind your own business. I suppose that would be like a Chinese speaking person saying, "I'm going to eat toes" instead of "toast". Learning to speak basic Chinese might not be so bad after all. At least it might keep me from getting into hot water.

Chapter Thirteen

On a few occasions, friends of Daddy Chen or Soo would drop in for tea. When my sister and I were first introduced to them, there were the usual smiles and greetings with chatter back and forth. When questions were directed to me, I would smile, nod, or respond with hilo (yes) one of the few words I had learned, hoping I was giving the right answer. When I was given a puzzled facial expression, I knew I'd given the wrong answer. True, I didn't understand the language, but I knew from the perplexed looks we got that the spoken words were about us. We were definitely the main topic of conversation for the evening.

I learned a few more new Chinese words when Chinese New Year rolled around—a time somewhere between January and February according to the Chinese calendar. During this special occasion the children were given little red envelopes called "lai see" after saying "Gong Hay Fat Choy" (wishing you great happiness and prosperity) to their parents, aunts, uncles, and any other visiting adults. These packets were filled with lucky money, to our glee. We were instructed to always thank the person with "doh jeh" and a Chinese name. All my parents' friends were called aunt or uncle even if they weren't a relative.

With the lai see envelopes handed to us, we were each given a pretty red zodiac calendar, which was like a booklet with the front cover adorned with different animals in a circle. Daddy Chen explained that the zodiac was similar to the western astrology. I recall seeing a page on astrology when I flipped through the Sun newspaper at home, but I was never interested in it. I was more anxious to get to the comic section where I could keep up on the life of Rex Morgan, Dagwood and Blondie, or Archie. I do recall a friend of Mom and Dad's who was interested in astrology. She mentioned that her sign was Aries which meant nothing to me.

In the Chinese zodiac there are twelve animals in the cycle: the rat, ox, tiger, rabbit, dragon, snake, horse, sheep, monkey, rooster, dog, and pig. Each animal represents a person's traits or qualities for the person born in the year of a specific animal. Just for fun we found the animal that coincided with our birth dates and what the animal represented. I was born in the Year of the Dragon. Apparently, the dragon is the mightiest of the animals. It symbolizes character traits such as dominance and ambition. Dragons prefer to live by their own rules and if left on their own, are usually successful. They're driven unafraid of challenges and willing to take risks. After thinking about all these qualities, I decided in some ways I was like a dragon, yet in other ways I was my own self. The remainder of the afternoon was spent amusing ourselves by finding the zodiac animals and traits of my sister. Unlike me, my sister had the traits of a sheep. She was gentle and calm. Eventually I realized that she was a faithful, fragile companion, a prime example of someone wiser and stronger than I could ever be.

The highlight of Chinese New Year was the Chinatown parade. There was the lion dance performance when a ferocious looking beast costumed in bright red and gold colours stomped through the street to a loud pounding drum beat and sharp clanging cymbals. A sharp curved horn protruding from its powerful head shook back and forth as the mighty animal pounced about in all directions. His long, curly eyelashes covered a pair of bright, wide eyes with each quick blink. I hid my face as the creature drew nearer. Somehow knowing how I felt, this mighty animal turned around and to the rhythm of the powerful beating drum danced energetically away.

Also dancing during the festival was the long dragon swaying from side to side as it pranced through the street. It was much longer than the lion and composed of several parts which were held up by men holding poles. This creature was blue and green and composed of parts of several different animals. A picture of the dragon with a thorough description of the enormous creature was given in the Chinese Times newspaper. It had the tail of a fish, the scales of a carp, the neck of a snake, the belly of a clam, the head of a camel, the claws of an eagle, the paws of a tiger, the ears of a cow, the eyes of a demon, and the beard of a goat.

I was told that dances for both the auspicious creatures were performed during festive occasions to chase away evil spirits and welcome in prosperous times. Though it was exciting to watch these mighty daring creatures, I hoped that the lion and dragon would keep on dancing down the street and not enter my imagination and dreams when nightfall approached.

Chapter Fourteen

Mom had packed a record, a deck of cards and a couple board games in our suitcase, knowing we loved to play games. Lin and I would pass time by playing Snap or Fish with the cards. When we were tired of cards, we would listen to a radio programme or our Alice in Wonderland record. Other days we would pull out our regular checkerboard or Chinese checkerboard for a change. Chinese Checkers was similar to regular checkers in some ways, only it was played with marbles on a starshaped board. The idea was to get your marbles to the other side of the board before your opponent. We thought checkers was a fun game.

One game I watched some of the grownups play was called Mahjong. It was a game somewhat like the card game Rummy which I'd seen played at home. Each player tried to form matched sets consisting of groups of three or four of a kind, or sequences of three or more cards of the same suit. Unlike Rummy, this Chinese game was played with ivory tiles with different pictures embossed on them. The tiles were adorned with pictures of different kinds of colourful flowers, Chinese characters, bamboo sticks or coins. I think the idea was to get matching suits. I didn't really understand the rules of the game but the clicking tiles and the loud chatter made it extremely noisy. It was here that I first heard the expression "aiyah" used in a loud, excited tone by the players. I realized that this word combined with a person's facial expressions was the outburst of one's hidden feelings. This was one time, Daddy Chen's persona which was one of complete composure became that of a boisterous man, blending with the rather raucous nature of the crowd around the table.

I eventually concluded that from the frowns on some faces, it meant "Oh oh!", "Oh no!", "Oh brother!", or "Oh rats!", while to those who seem to be having a lucky streak, the interjection probably meant "Yeah!", "Great!", "Wow!". I was always glad when this lively event was over and the person with the winning hand would lay down his tiles face up and with a smug look, shout "Sik Wu!" To the adults this was an enjoyable evening playing a fun game. To me with the shuffling of tiles and the loud chatter, it was a very loud night with a noisy game.

The only thing I looked forward to on these Mahjong nights were the treats we ate after the game was finished. All the earlier piercing racket was soon forgotten when a tray containing chu shiu bou, pork or shrimp dumplings, sweet little cakes, and fruit were served satiating my appetite.

On not such memorable occasions, I again heard the expression "aiyah" in the house. The word that made us stop in our tracks was used by grownups, including Daddy Chen and Soo whenever they were surprised, excited or disapproved of something. I once heard the phrase "ngo da nayge tou". I found out that although literally it means "I hit your head", I believe it would be equivalent to "you're going to get a spanking". It must have been used mostly on boys rather than girls. I don't think this interjection was ever directed towards me. But then, who knows.

Mom always wanted me to continue with piano lessons so Daddy Chen bought a piano. The piano book that my new piano teacher used contained popular rather than the classical pieces that I was used to but I didn't seem to mind. Practicing my piano exercises and new pieces was another way to keep me busy.

After eating Chinese meals daily, I recall telling Soo that she was a good cook. One day she offered to show me how to prepare some of the meals at which time I adamantly refused. However, when she was busily getting out the ingredients for our lunch or dinner, I would casually come closer to her, furtively peeking out of the side of my eye. There seemed to be a method to preparing the meal. Meat was sliced up thinly against the grain and vegetables were cut up. They were added to a frying pan of hot oil, thin slices of ginger, and garlic. When the food was cooked quickly over the hot flame, soya sauce was poured over it. Corn starch mixed with a little water was used with more sugar and soya sauce to thicken the sauce which was the final stage. Every meal had to include a pot of boiled rice. For a change we would have sticky rice with Chinese sausage and mushrooms which actually became one of my favourite dishes.

There were different soups that Soo made, the most common being egg drop soup with peas or mustard green soup. Then there were soups with what I call weird ingredients. I remember having fungus or seaweed in a soup. It looked and sounded worse than it tasted. One soup I wasn't anxious to try was called one-hundred-year-old egg soup. I didn't know that chickens lived to be one hundred years old. But then, maybe the eggs came from a dinosaur. I never did ask, and if I did, I don't recall being given an answer.

Anyway, I had always enjoyed making or baking recipes at home with Mom: soups, cookies, pies. Lin seemed to be getting along quite well in her new environment. So maybe it was time for me to relax a bit and become less of a grouch. That afternoon my sister and I made our first won ton soup, step by step. Soo made up the mixture of ground pork, sliced water chestnuts, fresh ginger, soy sauce, sesame oil, sliced scallions, and a little sugar. Then she pulled out the wrappers she'd bought in Chinatown. There was a certain way of folding the mixture which was spooned into the wrapper. The first few times we put too much or too little in the wrapper. To make the wrapper stick, you had to rub a bit of water around the edges. After a while, we got the knack of wrapping and by the time we'd finished, the last few wontons almost looked perfect. While we were wrapping the wonton, Soo boiled a large pot of water and a second pot with chicken broth, bok choy, and fresh ginger. Into the boiling water she would spoon about twelve won ton. After ten minutes she would scoop up the won ton with her ladle and pour them into a soup bowl with the broth. Sipping the delicious won ton soup was worth all the work. To make it more worthwhile, I had learned that I could be a little more cooperative, even smiling a bit, as we worked on something together.

Chapter Fifteen

I started my new school in the middle of grade six. I adjusted as well as can be expected. Because I now lived in a Chinese neighbourhood, most of the pupils at Beymar School were Chinese. I met new friends fairly quickly. They were Chinese but spoke English well. They could also understand and speak Chinese, which was an advantage I didn't have. I learned a new game that was played at recess or lunch time. I forget the Chinese name for it. We took a paper pom, pom, threw it into the air, bent one knee, then kicked the pom pom with the inside of one foot as many times as possible. The odd time, a smart aleck boy would come by, snatch the pom pom and do a few tricks with it, then disappear as quickly as he had appeared with a snicker on his face. The girls tuned me in on this annoying boy named Alex who would pester them whenever he had a chance. The next time he passed me with a smirk on his face I uttered, "Smart Aleck, Alex", just loudly enough for him to hear. I knew he had heard my remark as soon as he turned back and gave me a second look.

The next day the little twit purposely

strutted towards me with his two chums, Bobby and Douglas. Bobby introduced their pompous, haughty leader with "Meet our pal, Alex. His name is short for Alexander . . . you know, Alexander the Great, the mighty, skilled, smart leader. You three girls look timid enough to be his subjects."

That did it. I replied to their snooty remarks with, "Hi, Alexander the not-so-Great. My name is Carly. Talking about subjects, I bet the three of you were sleeping in class when the social studies teacher brought up the topic Alexander the Great. You forgot to mention that dear old Alexander came home fatigued and homesick after a battle in India with the great King Porus. Your buddies are as smart as you, Alexander. Not Porus (poor us). Poor you." They looked at each other not expecting my sarcastic response. My friends couldn't believe what had just occurred. Apparently, no one had stood up to these three know-it-alls before, especially a girl. I figured this would be the last we'd see of the three dimwits. I was wrong.

About a week later we ran into them in the school hallway. "Well, if it isn't the three Missketeers", one of them taunted, "Dopey, Hopey, and Mopey." I refused to let them get the upperhand so I retorted, "Birds of a feather flock together, don't they, birdbrains." Alex looked at me as he said, "You three are birds, too. You must be graceful doves. I heard you cooing." Just as I thought he wanted a truce, he started mimicking the peaceful bird. "Coo, coo, coo; cuckoo, cuckoo, You're a magician, too. Now you're a cuckoo bird." The three strutted off like proud turkeys. That was the final straw. They might have one this battle, but they hadn't won the war. This had turned into a real war . . . a war of the wits; a war with the three twits.

By now my hair had grown so long that it hung down my back. There were times I'd wear it in a pony tail so it wouldn't flop over the right side of my face. On the days I didn't have time to fiddle with it, when we were playing games at recess or lunchtime, strands of my loose hair which insisted on tickling my forehead got closer to my right eye. Before I knew it, I would sniff a couple times, with a quick sideways jerk of the head and a snappy pushback motion of my right hand, hoping the annoying hair would stay back where it belonged. The group of girls I usually hung around with noticed my strange habit. My best friend at Beymar was a tiny, bright, talented girl named Brenda who always seemed to know the correct answers in the science class. After school she went home and told her mother about my unusual habit to which her mother replied that it was just a tic.

The next day Brenda returned to school telling all her friends and me that I had a tic (tick). After looking up a picture of a tick in her Science book she described it as a tiny bug which feeds on blood. That made me freak out. I imagined a wingless, bloodsucking insect crawling through my hair, down my neck, across my shoulders, stopping under my armpits, then deciding to climb out and tumble down, landing on my striped ankle socks. I squirmed around, ferociously scratching my head and convulsively shaking my feet. I felt a tingling in my spine and suddenly a tickling on the vamp of my right foot. With a loud shriek, I jumped a mile high out of my desk seat and proceeded to throw off my sweater, shoes, and socks. Before disrobing any further, Mrs. Baker, who taught us grammar, yelled at the unruly class, waving her firm hand and within seconds you couldn't hear a pin drop . . . except for the sound of my rapidly moving feet as I jumped around like a dizzy diver on a spring board trying to avoid a colony of antsy bugs. Luckily the bell rang and the pupils, not wanting to waste a precious second of their playtime, headed towards the door, unaware that I was sitting on the floor, inspecting my feet.

Mrs. Baker questioned me in a soothing tone. After calming down, I explained the circumstances leading to my predicament. Mrs. Baker remarked that many children and adults have tics, but they don't necessarily last very long. "I'm sorry for all the trouble I caused in your classroom, Mrs. Baker." Her reply was, "Apology accepted, Carly. As a matter of fact, I owe you a big thank you. I hadn't decided what tomorrow's grammar lesson would focus on. Now I know. We'll review homonyms—words that sound the same but have different spelling and meanings." The next day when Mrs. Baker asked her classes to name as many homonyms as possible, the usual common words were given: to, two, too; wait, weight; hour, our. As I held up my hand and confidently called out the words "tic, tick" most of the pupils in the other classes asked what at least one of the words meant. Then my new word was added to the list. Now when I look up at the large round clock in the library, a big smirk comes over my face as I picture little bugs roaming around the numbers rhythmically to the tick-tick-ticking of the clock.

As for Alex and his two conniving buddies, their punishment was a week of detentions and writing one hundred lines of "I will behave in a respectable manner to all the girls". I blamed Alex for my misery. What I later found out was that the whole plan was instigated by his two buddies Bobby and Douglas. Douglas' mother had just opened a new sack of long grain fancy rice. Some of it fell out as she pulled the string at the top. Douglas, being a good helper that he was according to his mother, placed the rice that had fallen onto the floor into his pocket instead of the garbage can. It just so happened that the next day during gym time, we took off our shoes and socks to play a game on the slippery floor which had just been polished. This was the perfect time for Douglas to slip a few grains of rice into my socks which were under the wooden bench at the side of the locker room. The next day it was easy for Bobby who sat in the seat behind me in Mrs. Baker's room to reach up furtively at the opportune time and stealthily drop a few grains of rice on the collar of my blouse. Feeling something moving down my back, the unimaginable episode unfolded. Imagining there were ticks crawling, sliding and climbing on me, I jumped up and began shaking wild movements that appeared to be a cross between a panicky girl jitterbugging and leaping off of hot coals. While Douglas and Bobby held their stomachs from laughing so hard, Alex had a bewildered look on his face, but everyone was astonished at my outrageous, frenetic behaviour.

That is when Mr. Li, the vice-principal, walked in with a stern look on his face. "What's all this commotion?" he asked in a harsh tone. "I can hear you from my office." The class atmosphere was immediately as different as day and night. The three buddies and I were marched to his office where Mr. Li was determined to get to the bottom of this whole frenzied problem and to solve it one way or the other, and now. I had heard some pretty wild tales about Mr. Li. I never knew the correct pronunciation of his name. Some called him Mr. Li as in "igh" and others pronounced his name as Mr. Li as in "ee". Bobby mentioned that you dare not lie to Mr. Li or you'll be sorry. Douglas added he heard that the sticks on the drum kit in Mr. Li's office were meant for more than beating the drums. He saw a boy come out of the scary office crying his eyes out. He appeared to have black-and-blue marks on his leg. Bobby didn't bother mentioning that the limping boy had fallen off a jungle gym the day before.

As I followed the three hooligans reluctantly into the ominous room, there stood Mr. Li with his arms crossed, waiting to hear the boys' side of the story. After several questions, a nod, and sounds of hm-hm, uh-huh by the vice-principal between the ridiculous excuses of the first two culprits, finally, it was Alex's turn for an interrogation. He glanced at me shyly with the unexpected answer, "I was just trying to get the attention of the cute girl with long hair who had just moved to our school." After staring him in the eyes with my wide-opened mouth, I wasn't ticked off at all. As a matter of fact, when I thought about it, Alex was kind of cute, too.

The vice-principal gave me leeway in deciding the type of disciplinary action for the three mischief makers. Looking at their apologetic, forlorn faces, I said they should find books on bugs including ticks in the library and give a report to the class. I think these pranksters had finally learned their lesson. I calmly left with a "Thank you, Mr. Li" (Lee). After telling Mr. Li how sorry they were for their naughty tricks, the boys trotted out behind me with drooping heads and shoulders, expressing their apologies to me and their gratitude to an understanding man of authority. With respect, the boys and I all agreed that the handling and solution to this turbulent situation was done in a fair way, a kind way, known only by us as the Lee way. Determined to have the last say, I wittily added, "And that's no lie."

When the three o'clock bell rang, Brenda and I walked out of the school together. As we passed one of the trees laden with beautiful fall leaves, one of them drifted through the air, landing right on the top of my head. Feeling something light moving around in my hair, I quickly reached up with my right hand to brush it away. Brenda interrupted my motion and words of hysteria by calmly whispering, "It's just a leaf." Then we both chuckled and left the school yard.

Chapter Sixteen

After that, clocks took on different meanings. I found the large clock in my homeroom had a mesmerizing effect on me. Instead of spending silent reading time usefully or working on a writing assignment, I caught myself daydreaming. I'd find myself back in my old neighbourhood. There was my old, wooden-shingled house with the large boulevard in the front. I was among my friends chatting or playing. The strange thing is that not one of them had ever noticed my quirks, what I now know as tics. If they had, there was never a mention of them. And now that I think about it, I hadn't noticed my friends' habits either. The more I thought about it, the more I realized that all of us or most of us have brief and sudden movements that we aren't aware of: Tommy had a habit of eye-blinking when he was up to bats; Billy would clear his throat before responding to a question; Peter would snort and honk when blowing his nose; Aila had a bad habit of chewing her nails; and now I find out that I did a lot of sniffing combined with pushing my hair off my forehead. Nobody noticed; nobody cared. To us, all that really mattered was that we were a close-knit group of friends who shared common interests, who cared about each other, regardless of our faults, regardless of our tics.

The bell rang, jolting me back to reality. I was now in a new school with new friends. At Beymar, besides Chinese pupils born in Canada, there were also New Canadian students from China who attended. I remember someone saying that Chinese kids born in Canada were referred to as bananas, which didn't seem very nice to me. Any derogatory term spoken to another person was wrong. Besides, if anything, I was more like an Anjou pear: green when it came to understanding the Chinese culture, having a torso shaped like a pear being thin at the top and gradually extending to my overly wide hips, and my inner core being white.

The following days and weeks at school became more enjoyable. I found some classes more interesting and enjoyable than others. I had always liked music and found it fun learning to play the recorder or taking a turn at beating on a drum. Peter was known as a latecomer who would always be the last boy into a classroom. His last excuse that his saxophone weighed him down didn't go over very well since that was one instrument that hadn't been introduced to us yet. I had heard by the grapevine that he no longer played the flute because of Mr. Hornsby's comment that he should quit while he was ahead. It was said in a joking manner, but being rather serious Peter had taken it the wrong way. I tried to give Peter some moral support by telling him that sometimes it's best to laugh things off. I told him about my experience. I was terrible when it came to drawing. When Mr. Scribbs saw my drawing of an umbrella, he said he'd never seen Mary Poppins floating through the sky holding a mushroom. That didn't stop me from working on my art skills. I still can't draw worth beans, but I didn't give up. Peter thought about it and agreed. Laughing is much better than sulking. Besides, he was enjoying the recorder and a couple of kids thought he sounded really good. As a matter of fact, before he left, Mr. Hornsby suggested that one day Peter might like to try the flute since he'd improved immensely with the recorder. Peter just smiled even though he knew Mr. Hornsby's hearing hadn't improved at all. I had heard, too, that Mr. Hornsby's hearing wasn't what it used to be. Students would give him strange looks when he didn't respond to their question or gave up after hearing the word pardon repeated five times. Either the music teacher's hearing was eventually getting worse or he purposely tuned out the cacophony of instruments played by his persistent beginner band, usually followed by the hoots and cackles of the odd player. After listening to the band, I was more understanding of Mr. Hornsby's actions. I wonder if the wailing sound I heard came from him or the music pupils. I was happy to hear that Mr. Hornsby, who now had gray tufts scattered on his bald head, was planning to retire that June. After his thirty years of teaching music, he deserved a relaxing life in a peaceful atmosphere.

Mrs. Baker had not been feeling very well the last couple of months. She began taking the odd day off, which was strange for her since she rarely missed a day of school even when she came to school sneezing and blowing her nose. That was the time we wished Mrs. Baker had stayed home because it was the beginning of most of us coming down with a cold. We didn't miss her too much because her regular substitute was a handsome young man named Mr. Emmy whose personality was almost the opposite of Mrs. Baker's. He handled the class in a firm, but kind, understanding way. This curly-haired, brown-eyed fellow also made his lessons informative and interesting. His quick remarks and joking manner had the class laughing and everyone's attention. The last time Mr. Emmy returned he announced that Mrs. Baker had taken a leave-of-absence, whatever that meant, and he'd been requested to continue teaching us until the end of the year. The class showed its approval by its loud cheer. Although Mrs. Baker would be missed, I figured she needed to rest and maybe change her diet since she'd gained noticeable weight the last couple of months.

One morning Mr. Emmy announced that our topic would be on the subject of etymology. That was a new word that I hadn't heard before. "Can anyone tell me the definition of etymology?" Mr. Emmy inquired. Not one hand was raised. By the blank looks on the faces, I figured I wasn't the only one who'd never heard this long word before. We took out our dictionaries and thumbed through the pages until we found the word. Sarah Wong raised her hand quickly to which Mr. Emmy called out, "Miss Wong, would you please read the meaning of etymology for the class." She confidently uttered, "Etymology: the study of the origin and history of words, or a study of this type relating to one particular word."

"Thank you, Miss Wong. You're absolutely wight (right). Miss Wong is rarely wong (wrong)", he added jokingly. Sarah held her head up high. Then he looked at me. "Miss Chen, I see you had your hand up, too. I'll let you answer the next question. Keep your Chen (chin) up." This time as I looked around, I knew the laughter was not at me, but at Mr. Emmy's play on words. I think he deserved an Emmy. For a change I wanted to outsmart Mr. Emmy with a last word on the subject. I smugly said, "Mr. Emmy, you deserve an Emmy for your humour and play on words." I had no sooner spurted out my words when the boy sitting across the aisle from me interjected, "But my first name is Oscar. I'm entitled to an Oscar." From then on others in the classroom participated with their thoughts. What might have been a boring lesson on etymology turned out to be one of fascination and interest. One last question was about to be thrown at the class. Saved by the bell, the lesson was concluded by the suggestion that we look up the etymology of last names. As the students promptly headed towards the door, Mr. Emmy called out, "Nice work, Carly! Your input made this lesson on etymology lots of pun." With a quick wink from him, I joined the rest of the smiling class, knowing this had been the beginning of a great day.

Chapter Seventeen

As the days whisked by, without realizing it, I was no longer seen as the new girl at school. I was just part of the regular group of grade six students. We were all slowly changing in our attitudes and appearances. Even the BAD group (Billy Alex Douglas) had dispersed and had become much more responsible. Their energy was spent on school sports rather than taunting the girls. After noticing their high interest and skills in basketball, the three of them became members of one of the Beymar basketball teams known as the Challenging Chargers, a name quite befitting for them. There were two other basketball teams in the school, but after losing several games to them it was the Challenging Chargers that was associated with Beymar's basketball team. To root them on, a group of girls formed a cheerleader's club. I helped to create the lyrics for all the cheers, and before I knew what happened, I became one of the cheerleaders to encourage and cheer them on. Money was raised for both cheerleaders' and basketball players' uniforms through cupcake days, cookie days, penny days, and wishing well days. Also, the PTA donated money towards the worthy cause.

A new class added to this year's curriculum was a woodwork class. It sounded like lots of fun, getting to handle carpentry tools and build things. Mrs. Shoemaker was our teacher. She chortled as she told us her name. I'm Mrs. Shoemaker but I don't make shoes, I build wooden furniture. Then she held up and named the basic tools that we'd be using: a hammer, tape measure, carpenter's pencil, nail puller. Next, she showed us the pieces of wood we'd be using for our first project. When she asked us what else we needed, no one put up their hands. Well, how do you expect your project to stay together? When she held up a bottle of glue, we all laughed and together yelled, "With nails!"

Before beginning our first of several projects, we learned the techniques of holding and using a hammer. I found out that hammering a nail into a piece of wood wasn't as easy as it looks. Each time I tried to hammer my nail I would miss the head. After several failed attempts, I stared at the head of the little nail and with my hammer and extra energy gave it a good swing. Wham! My strike and bellow was an announcement that I had hit the nail, but the wrong one . . . it was the nail on the middle finger of my left hand. I didn't feel quite as badly when I heard the ouches, moans, and groans of others in the room. This was our first lesson in the woodwork class. As we headed out of the room, my eyes were drawn to a large poster above the doorway. On it was a fantasy picture of characters in a magical setting. Underneath was the beginning of a motto which read "Building my _____". We were to complete the motto with our own thought. After pondering on those words, I realized it could be taken by each of us in our own way. After all, each of us had characteristics, talents, backgrounds, and experiences that made us what we are: unique and continually changing.

After a few months we became quite adept at using the hammer. Each of the grade six woodwork classes were given the task of building a small wooden wishing well for their homeroom. It didn't take long before the donations made by the teachers, parents and pupils in the classroom filled the wishing wells. Each time I dropped a penny, nickel, or dime into the well I made a wish. Sometimes I wished that I was better in math and science; sometimes my wish was that the Charging Challengers would win against the opposing school team; sometimes I wished that something would occur to make me happier; mostly I wished that Lin would be healthy and we could go back home.

The cheerleaders gathered at lunchtime and after school to practise the cheers and moves. I taught them a couple of my created cheers and asked for more ideas on catchy cheers and dance moves.

You could hear us practising the cheers:

1,2,3,4, Who's going to get the score
Challenging Chargers!
Challenging Chargers!
YEAH! YEAH! YEAH!
Red white and gold
Challenging Chargers
Mighty and bold!
Watch them let off steam
This unbeatable team,
Challenging Chargers!
Challenging Chargers!
YEAH! YEAH! YEAH!

We practised moving our arms, legs, and bodies into all kinds of positions: stretching, squatting, turning, constantly shaking and twirling our pom poms, and hopping to the sides using various synchronized moves while we chanted our lyrics. By the time our session was over, our weak voices and aching arms and legs were ready for a rest. But we felt good about our achievements that day.

When the opposing teams in our school played against each other, we would begin cheers for the Challenging Chargers while the team playing against ours that day would chant the lyrics for their team. The enthusiastic spectators sitting on the side bleachers joined in the cheers as they rooted for their favourite team. It was a great time to have fun and display sportsmanship.

Once a week all the students gathered in the auditorium where important issues were brought up. First of all, we always stood up to sing our country's national anthem "O Canada". We then discussed various items on the agenda. Sometimes the topic of school rules would be led by Mr. Harding; other times we were informed of future school events; there were also times when outstanding pupils or groups were recognized for their hard work or achievements. At one of our auditorium days a grade six student named Lai Kay Lee performed for us. She played Beethoven's Fur Elise on the piano. Her nimble fingers moved quickly over the keys as she played effortlessly and majestically. After closing the session with "God Save Our King" the classes marched out of the large gymnasium in orderly fashion. My mind was still on Lai Kay. Suddenly I saw myself in her place. I had a vivid picture of myself performing before the whole school. If only, I could play half as beautifully as she did. Watching her play was enough motivation for me to practise and play the piano more seriously from that day forward. It was also another way to keep my mind on the present rather than always on the past.

Chapter Eighteen

Before long the cool, rainy days of autumn were replaced by the cold, frosty days of winter. Then came the long-awaited day. The eyes of school kids brightened up as light powdery snowflakes drifted silently from the sky, landing against the cold, glass window panes. Knowing our concentration had been interrupted, we were given the last ten minutes of the day as free time. At our last auditorium day Mr. Harding, the principal, had suggested that we think of new activities to play in the snow at recess and lunchtime since throwing snowballs at each other had been banned due to someone's injury to an eye and complaints of headaches after being hit in the head by a hard snowball. Ginny suggested Puff ball where you threw a snowball into an outdoor basketball net. One boy suggested that we make igloos. The majority of the class liked Gordon's idea of Snowdragon. Two teams were formed to make dragons. The idea was to tag the last person in the lineup which was the dragon's tail.

The weather forecast had predicted snow for the next two weeks. I participated in different activities while there was snow on the ground. The only drawback to the snowdragon game was that I was covered with snow from head to foot. I was able to shake off much of the snow on my jacket, but after school it was no fun putting my feet into boots that were full of water from melted snow. I took them off as soon as I got home and made sure they were dry and warm for the next time I needed them.

February was upon us before the blink of an eye. The kids were looking forward to the annual dress up on Valentine's Day. At my former school we dressed up for Hallowe'en but never for Valentine's Day. Some of the mothers offered to make cookies or little cupcakes, Others offered to provide juice, and Miss Long brought some tiny, red, valentine-shaped candies. Betsy described some of the costumes worn by students in the past—cupid, a Valentine card, a chocolate bunny, a white pantsuit with red hearts scattered on it—but nobody had ever been disguised as a Valentine clown which I decided to be. I already had a curly, red wig and cherry nose from previous Hallowe'ens on my closet shelf. I thought of clothes I had at home that could be used in my clown outfit. The morning of the special day I put on my bulky vest, and pair of jeans. On top of the vest I put an old shirt. Over the jeans, I pulled on a pair of pink sweatpants with coloured stickers randomly stuck on them and a pair of suspenders to hold the pants up. Soo's eye liner, make up and lipstick were smeared all over my face. Around my neck was a red string holding up a heart-shaped card that read "Don't laugh when I ask you to BE MY VALENTINE".

My sister Lin was dressed as a lady bug. Together we strolled hand in hand as we looked forward to an awesome day with its fun events and activities. As we turned the corner at Jackman Street, Lin spotted Alex walking towards us. "Hi, Alex!" she called out getting his attention. "Oh, no", I muttered. "Now he knows who's under the disguise." Instead he inquired, "Where's your sister today?" I couldn't believe my ears when Lin replied, "She's sick today so my cousin offered to take me to school." Alex chortled as he took my hand and said, "I'll walk you to school this morning, Lin. Your cousin can stay a few steps behind us in case we're walking too fast for her, I mean him." He gave me a wink and the two of them proceeded to walk at a relaxing pace as I dragged myself behind them. When we arrived at the school, the girls looked at Lin and then Alex wondering where I was. As I walked into the school unnoticed, Alex told them I wasn't feeling well so he offered to bring Lin to school today. Lin played along with the joke and they both went on their way.

This was going to be a real fun day. As I went into our homeroom, I secretly told Mrs Yee who I was. She told the class that a new boy had transferred into our school and perhaps this was Jay Chow, the new student. She added,

"Thank you for dressing up, Jay. I think your Valentine clown costume is unique", to which the class clapped their approval. I recognized everyone else in their costumes and disguises, but nobody could guess who I was. They thought I was probably the new pupil. Some of them thought I was Bing who was the chubbiest boy in the school. Others weren't sure, but no one guessed who the clown was. About an hour later, I started to feel warm. From then on things got stifling hot. I asked to be excused a few times. When I reached the girls' washroom, I'd take off my wig and shirt for a breather. After fanning myself with the wig, I'd put the disguise back on and traipse back to my room. I was hoping the make up wouldn't run. If it did, it would look as if the laughing clown was crying which I'd probably be doing by the end of the day. Throughout the day I casually suggested to each teacher that the window or door be opened since fresh air was good for our concentration.

When it was gym time, we were unable to play volleyball in case our costumes got ruined. Instead we opted for a talent show since some of the boys were starting to clown around. "No more clowning around!" I said in a teacher's rebuking tone. When I had everyone's attention, I took three rubber balls out of a cloth bag that had been hanging over my shoulder and began my juggling act which I'd been practising at home for a couple of weeks. The kids were amazed and applauded as I tossed the balls into the air, catching one at a time and throwing them higher and higher until one of the balls left the orderly path and bonked one of the onlookers on his head. As I tried to retrieve the lost ball, the other two bounced around like dancing springs—boing, boing—until the second one bopped Johnny on the nose and the third one came to a halt in Janet's little wicker basket which contained some of her mother's homemade valentine cookies. I ran over to Janet, comforting her before her sniffling turned into a crying event. By then, Miss Pollinger quietened the raucous onlookers by telling them she would demonstrate her skills at gymnastic. The patient gym teacher thanked me for my entertaining performance and said, "Well, clowns are supposed to make children laugh, and you did a good job of that."

I was so relieved when the lunch bell rang. I could hardly wait for my sweltering body to feel the cool breeze. I was about to join the girls when they told me I belonged with the boys. I finally succumbed and gave away my secret telling them who I really was to which they just laughed at me. I'd become hoarse from trying to disguise my Carly voice into a husky boyish one. Finally, I took off my wig so my friends could see my long dangling hair. They thought I was hilarious and had tricked everyone. Brenda chuckled as she said, "You even tricked me, Carly. What a clown!"

We had an extended recess in order for

the students who were not yet in costumes to change. We would then have a parade, a judging contest in which the judging panel was made up of teachers and some of the parents, and a Valentine's party. The event would run through lunchtime and continue until the end of the school day.

When the bell rang, the students scurried back filling their rooms with characters that I hadn't imagined. There were Disney characters, movie characters, comic characters, and you name it. Douglas was dressed as Spiderman which suited him to a T and Bobby decided to be Luke Skywalker since he was a fan of the Star Wars movies; Oscar looked cute in his Yoda outfit. All the costumes had a touch of pink or red, or a little heart; anything that reminded us it was a Valentine's Day theme. The girls looked magical in their fairy tale costumes. There were fairies, cupids, girls in fancy skirts and dresses, all reminding us of this special, exciting event. Brenda, with her loose, white dress and wig with braids at the side and a valentine necklace made a perfect Princess Leia. Molly was dressed like Cinderella in a sweet white dress trimmed with red hearts on a gold ribbon. I thought she needed a Prince Charming to . . . Before I could finish my thought, in walked Alex in a dignified manner that made my heart beat like a drum. He was more than a Prince Charming; he was a King of Hearts . . . my heart. Why couldn't I have thought of being a fairy, an angel, a princess, or a queen? Here I was, a silly old clown, making a fool of myself. If Alex was the King of Hearts in a deck of cards. I was the Joker. Why didn't I think of being the Queen of Hearts instead of a ridiculous old clown? A day that started out as a fun day turned out to be one of misery, a complete disaster. I might have made everyone else laugh except myself. I guess the joke was on me.

After school, I hurried to Lin's room and took her hand. I told her we'd take a different route home. I didn't want to run into Alex for fear of showing my embarrassment. As we walked along the sidewalk parallel to our usual street, Lin turned her head to the right just in time to see Alex. Excitedly she yelled, "Alex!" With a subdued no I yanked her hand hoping Alex was deaf in his left ear. Turning his head Alex shouted back, "Hey, what are you two doing on that street? Are you already tired of the scenery over here?" I saw him rushing towards us so there was no use trying to hide. I knew I was blushing from embarrassment when Alex commented that I must still be hot from my two layered clown costume. To make matters worse, along came Jack still dressed up as Jack of hearts. He was such a card, always trying to impress the girls with his snide remarks. "I think you make a perfect joker, Carly, and a wild one at that. The next time I play cards you can come on deck", he snorted. He had to get in his two cents worth. "Okay, Mr. Smarty Pants",

I thought to myself. Deciding not to show my vengeful spirit, I nonchalantly said, "You're all heart, Jack. Jack be nimble, Jack be quick, Jack jump over the candlestick." In my head the added words rang, and I hope you knock over the candlestick and burn your toes. Feeling a bit of remorse at my thoughts, I knew I still had a long way to go to improve my attitude, but so did Jack. Then my loving sister interrupted our witty but sarcastic conversation by saying she was my fairy godmother and with a touch of her magic wand could make me into a queen of hearts. Alex looked at me with a twinkle in his eye and softly said, "'King and Queen of Hearts' sounds like a perfect match to me." Picturing myself in an elegant gown fit for a queen with a king by my side, I continued on my way home feeling dignified and gracious, and striving to be kinder, loving and more forgiving.

Chapter Nineteen

The days of each season moved by as if a person had pushed the fast motion button. Autumn and winter had unfurled before my eyes. Now the days were getting longer and warmer, a sign that spring was on its way. Previous school activities continued and outdoor activities were added to the schedule. Boys and girls joined the baseball and soccer teams while activities such as indoor basketball continued. By now the Charging Challengers were the top team at Beymar after winning the majority of basketball games. They practised longer hours now since the announcement was broadcast over the PA system that there was going to be a tournament between schools from all lower mainland districts. Not only did this mean more hours of practice for the Challenging Charger team but also for their cheerleaders. The team practised their basic drills repeatedly. Some of them included shooting, dribbling, and passing at accelerated speeds. Mr. Brown, the basketball coach also reviewed helpful tactics when it came to rebound and defence. He was an outstanding coach. With the knowledge he'd shared with the boys, the probability that these incredible, unbeatable players would win against any school basketball team was easily 2 to 1. There was no doubt in my mind that the Challenging Chargers would be this year's winning team; but then, I'm a little biased.

The cheerleaders practised daily for a half hour at lunchtime and about forty-five minutes after school besides any spare time they could gather. I had to be home before four o'clock in order to arrive at Chinese School on time.

Like most Chinese kids I went to Chinese school in Chinatown after English school. I remember climbing steep stairs to my classroom which was in a tall old building. I was twelve years old which made me the oldest and biggest student in my grade one class. At Kon Mung, the students learned to read, write, and speak Chinese. We were given soft-covered Chinese books with Chinese characters which were written/read from top to bottom, right to left. I found it quite easy memorizing the lines in my two books. I can hear myself reading from one of the books – siu siu, mou; siu siu, mou; siu siu mou; tiu, tiu, tiu. If I remember correctly, it translated little little cat; little little cat; little little cat; jump, jump, jump.

The other book was not as colourful and didn't have pictures. The first sentence I learned from this brown book was "ngo moon dick hawk how", the translation being "our school". Saying and writing the days of the week consecutively was just as easy since all one needed to do was add the numbers from one to six after the word "li bi". I remember learning the numbers when I went to Saturday Chinese classes back home. Monday was libi yut; Tuesday was libi ye, Wednesday was libi sum, and so on.

Reading and memorizing the words was a fairly easy task. Writing the characters was a bit tricky. Using a Chinese pen brush and ink was quite different from using a pencil or pen that I was accustomed to using. First we were taught to hold the Chinese brush vertically with our ring finger, middle finger, and thumb to hold the brush upright. Then we dipped the brush into the black ink and keeping our elbow on the desk we proceeded to write strokes in a specific order. Writing the numbers from one to three was easy since number one was a horizontal line written from left to right; number two was two horizontal lines and number three was three horizontal lines. Number four was a little trickier. It looked like a window with curtains. That's when we had to learn to do strokes in a specific order. Some of them were slightly slanted vertical lines, some were slightly slanted horizontal lines, some were curved, some were dots. The characters became more complicated as time went on. The hardest character for me to learn to write was my Chinese name Lai Ling. After much practice I mastered it, considering it quite a feat.

Each day we learned to read, write, and

repeat lines by rote. There was no conversational Chinese which would have been an advantage. But I think the teacher took for granted that all the students could speak some Chinese which they would use at home. At the end of the year I was presented with a certificate. The teacher made a speech, probably congratulating us and saying what a privilege it had been teaching us and telling what a hardworking, obedient class we had been. I smiled and received my award graciously even though I didn't understand a word spoken to me as I proudly received my first-year Chinese school certificate.

Well, now I can count from one to ten in a few languages: Finnish which I learned from my playmate who lives on Charles St., Japanese which I learned from a playmate on Keefer St., Chinese which I learned during lessons from the Chinese pastor and reviewed at Kon Mung Chinese School, and of course my first language which is English.

My Japanese friend, Kina, took me to a large park not far from where we lived. Half of it was covered with grass while the other part was a playground where one could play baseball. Sometimes she and her family would watch her dad and friends play with a boomerang. I'd never seen one close up and didn't know how it worked. Kina described the boomerang and how it worked. It was a curved tool that when thrown correctly, would fly in a curve rather than a straight line, so it would always return to its starting point. M-m-m, I thought to myself. I wonder if I'm like a boomerang. Whenever I go somewhere, I want to go back to where I started. I wonder if I'll ever return to the place that I first started.

Chapter Twenty

Although outwardly we appeared to be adjusting to our new environment, we missed Mom and Dad so much. Even when we were among people, I was lonely. We were not permitted to contact Mom or Dad. When things became too heavy on my heart, I would secretly phone Mom. I can only imagine how hard it would have been for her. She wanted to be sure we were happy and safe. One time she came to my new school to see us. I saw her walking down the steps of one of the additions to the old school. She had been talking with my sister's teacher to see how we were adjusting to our new environment. It would put her mind at ease to know that we were safe and happy. We were safe and as happy as could be expected. Another time when I phoned her from a girlfriend's house, we arranged to meet Mom at Third Beach. I planned the details carefully as to the day and time my friends, sister and I would go swimming. When I saw Mom, I wanted so badly to take her gentle hand and go home with her, and I know she felt the same way.

Then an unexpected opportunity came

for me to see Mom and hopefully some of my friends from the old neighbourhood. Beymar had climbed to the top two basketball teams in the district. There were two teams left in the playoffs: Beymar and Sir Arnold Johnson. It would be playing against my old school, the one where I had spent the first six years of my childhood days until my sister and I had been taken away.

In my head I plotted as to a way I could contact Mom, letting her know my school basketball team would be playing against Sir John Arnold in two weeks. I wondered if it would be possible for her and some of my friends to be at the game. I'd then make arrangements for all of us to meet. I asked my good friend Brenda if I could use her phone again when I went to her house after school to which she always agreed. I could hardly wait for the day to come. I practised cheerleading even more enthusiastically and longer at school, at a friend's house, at home, and on the way to and from home. About a week before the big day, I felt a cold coming on. My throat was a bit sore so I gargled salt and water to soothe it. The next day my voice became a bit raspy. I tried to use it as little as possible except for our cheerleader practices. On the third day the unthinkable occurred. I had laryngitis. When I opened my mouth, all you could hear was a croak or a little squeak. Two days before the game when I opened my mouth all you could hear was a whisper. The nurse told me I should stay at home and rest my voice which wasn't a solution to my problem. She then advised me to keep hydrated and drink lots of fluids. I could suck on menthol candies to sooth my throat, and I could continue gargling salt water. Her suggestions were helpful, but not good enough to solve my problem. Nobody wanted a voiceless cheerleader. Unfortunately, everyone agreed that I would have a replacement for the first competition. I couldn't believe it. I guess this was my punishment for being such a sneaky conniver.

Time healed my voice and temperament. I probably felt worse than anyone, so I thought. I was told that there would be another opportunity. Everything works out for my good even when things don't seem, to be going my way. When I found out that Beymar didn't defeat Sir John Arnold, I blurted out, "Oh no!" I felt much better when I heard the news that Sir John Arnold hadn't defeated Beymar either. The score was a tie so a second game would be held at Sir John Arnold with the hopes that the tie would be broken. I was in my glory when the announcement was made that the two teams would compete in a month's time. By then I was sure to be over this wretched laryngitis. The words that I had heard on other occasions echoed in my head. There's a purpose for all things, and all things work together for good. As I pondered on these words, I began to understand that time and experiences can have a strong influence on a person. Maybe I needed to change a little. Although I was determined, I could be less stubborn, more patient, a little kinder, and more understanding among a few other changes in my attitude and nature, just like . . . and before my eyes appeared my little sister. Smiling, we took each other's hand and strolled home to the big house on Keefer Street.

Chapter Twenty-One

Busily doing my daily chores, activities and schoolwork, the day I'd been looking forward to was suddenly upon me. Again, I'd schemed to meet my family and my friends at the basketball tournament. This was going to be an emotional day for me. I boiled over with fervidness. Four pupils from each of the grade 4, 5, and 6 classes were chosen by the teachers and rewarded for their good citizenship. Lin was one of the four pupils in her grade 4 class who had the honour to be accompanied by a volunteer teacher and ride along with the players and cheerleaders with their escorting teachers.

As we approached Sir John Arnold School I almost broke down as past memories and feelings aroused my emotions. Then the moment we'd been hoping and waiting for arrived. There stood my smiling Mom holding onto my brother's arm, walking towards me. Right behind them were my sisters and some of my old neighbourhood friends. With ardour, everyone crowded around us, the centre of attention. The hugs, kisses, and excitement from the inquisitive group and replies from each of us as to the events in our lives the past year and a half were interrupted by a loud voice on the speaker announcing that the game would be starting in ten minutes. The cheerleaders from Johnson School had already begun chanting and stepping to their cheers. In all the excitement I'd completely forgotten I was part of my team's cheerleaders. Just then, Bertha, the captain of my group called my name as she grabbed me and told me to make a quick change from my dull sweat pants to my bright cheer leader's uniform. I madly pulled the red top embossed with our school's name in shiny gold letters over my head and put on the short white pleated skort. Then we rushed to our side of the gym, grabbed our pom poms and with the rest of the girls dashed to the middle of the gym where we performed some of the cheers and dance moves that we had practised for so many hours. As we performed our cheers, at times the din of the crowd almost drowned us out. When a player scored, the crowd, roared. Only once was there a hushed atmosphere as the spectators waited for a successful attempt by one of Beymar's players to throw the ball into the hoop due to a foul. Watching the enthused spectators as they yelled and participated with such ardour was worth every minute. The first part of the game finished with a click on the scoreboard: Beymar 43 Arnold 41

After a fifteen-minute break, the players on both teams were refreshed and with restored energy stormed back onto the floor ready for the next quarter period. As usual there was an atmosphere filled with raucous until the unimaginable happened. Two players collided in the air as they fought for the basketball. One was Billy; the other was Alex. Stunned for a few seconds, Alex wavered as he rose from the floor. Billy didn't rise. He lay on the cold floor motionless. Before long, two paramedics came. Billy was quickly rushed to the hospital in the high low wailing ambulance with its flashing red light.

The game had to continue regardless of the waning momentum of the crowd due to the mishap. With diminished enthusiasm both games played the last quarter. Limping Alex being substituted by Jay for the remainder of the game sat on the side bench. Beymar won the tournament, but the expected roaring hip hoo hurrahs were replaced by a quieter yeah and clapping as the line of rival players shook hands with the opposing team.

The Beymar basketball team and onlookers headed towards the school bus. After making my round of hugs and goodbyes to Mom, my siblings and all my old neighbourhood friends, we hopped onto the bus. I looked around, spotting Alex, who had just joined his players with a forlorn look not at all one holding the position of the top star player whose team was now ranked as number one. I think I knew why.

Like Alex, the next two weeks pervaded

my mind with the game and of Billy who was still in the hospital. My Aunt Betty and Uncle Tom usually dropped by our place once a month. From our place, they were planning on heading to Burnaby to visit Uncle Tom's brother. I meekly asked him if he'd be going by the Burnaby Hospital to which he replied that his brother didn't live far from it. I told him about my friend Billy in the hospital and I was anxious to see him. Uncle Tom was only too happy to oblige. My aunt and uncle would drop me off and pick me up in a couple of hours as they were on their way home. That would be just perfect.

Billy was sitting up, sipping a drink of milk when I tiptoed into his room, hoping he'd finished his nap. With a surprised look on his face, I greeted him warmly and tried to say cheery words. He seemed excited to see me. I remembered how he was a collector of basketball cards but afraid he might already have it, I brought a basketball shaped eraser. I could tell he was extremely pleased with my choice. "Thanks, Carly. It's great. I need one to erase all my spelling mistakes." We both chuckled at his remark. Then enthusiastically he added, "Alex was here a couple of days ago. He brought me the latest basketball card which I didn't have." As Billy showed me the card, I found out a lot about Alex which Billy had learned from their visit together at the hospital.

Alex was from a family of four. About two

years ago his mother, father, younger sister, and he were on their way home from a Chinatown parade. As they were crossing the street, a car swerved into the crowd of pedestrians, hitting his family. Only Alex survived. Apparently, the driver was an old man who'd suffered a heart attack. From that day on, Alex's new home was with his grandmother whom he called Popo. Alex then became friends with Bobby and Douglas who gave him the support he needed. Both of them knew what it was like to lonely. Both of them knew how good it felt to have the support of a friend. Bobby was raised by a single mother, and Douglas was raised by an Aunt and Uncle. They both had people who loved them, but spent long hours working. They had all faced times of loneliness, but now there was someone to fill those lonely hours. The three boys became close buddies who vowed to stick together in all kinds of weather. They would always be there to support one another. After hearing Billy's story of Alex and the two boys' backgrounds, I had a different perspective of each of them. This explained a lot of things about those three mischievous boys, I mean those three boys who used to be mischievous. They brought to mind the proverb "a friend in need is a friend indeed".

Alex gave his favourite basketball card to Billy which was an admirable deed. Knowing how much that picture of Markus Christon, the famous basketball star was to Alex prompted me to write a letter to him explaining what had happened. It was on the radio and in the newspaper that his arrival in Vancouver would be sometime in May. My eyes almost popped out when our school received the mail from Markus Christon informing us that an appearance would be made on May 26th by the star. On that day Marcus Christon had a captive audience as he spoke of his childhood dream to become a basketball player and how his persistence paid off. On the court he showed us a few of his entertaining strategic moves. Before signing autographs for all the mesmerized pupils, he announced that he had a special autographed picture for Alex Lee, the boy who had so selflessly given his card of the popular player to his friend in the hospital. As Alex rose to receive the cherished picture, questioning in his head how this famous player heard about his actions, he shook hands with the basketball icon. His thank you was drowned by the boisterous cheers and clapping of the excited pupils. As I joined in with the Beymar pupils, I had a warm feeling for this deserving boy.

Chapter Twenty-Two

There were two months left in our days at Beymar. After completing our final tests, our days were filled with practising for Sports Day, going on field trips, inviting entertainment groups, and having volunteers including parents who were willing to teach us a few basic skills such as cooking and baking for the girls while the boys learned more advanced woodwork.

Our first lesson on baking was given by Molly's and Betsy's mothers. Their job was to teach us how to make sugar cookies. I figured it would be easy since I'd helped Mom make cookies and cakes for special days and when we were expecting to have company. This was going to be easy. Mrs. Chin taught us the names of the common baking utensils and the ingredients we'd need for the cookies. She pointed to the wooden spoon, hand mixer, electric mixer, measuring spoons and cups, mixing bowl, rolling pin, and cookie pans. I already knew that most cookies and cakes started with sugar and butter; next you added a beaten egg and vanilla; finally, you mixed the dry ingredients consisting of flour, sugar, baking powder or baking soda, and added them to the wet mixture. This was going to be a piece of cake, I mean cookies. I could even help my classmates, especially if they'd never baked before.

In groups of four, each of us worked together in measuring the ingredients correctly in the spoons and cups before mixing. As we took turns stirring the batter each with a wooden spoon. I remarked, "This is a tedious method of stirring. Using a hand mixer would be much quicker." I boasted, "I'll show you how it's done the modern way." I took the hand mixer and displayed my experience beginning the mixer at a low speed in the thick batter. Moving the setting to the next level, the beaters began whizzing around faster hitting some of the chunks I'd missed. For a second the uncontrollable hand mixer scooped up the batter. Meaning to lower the speed, I pushed it to the Level 3 which was even faster. The beaters jumped around hitting a few chunks in the gucky batter causing the gooey mixture to splatter onto Bertha's black hair which was now streaked with white and purple and drenching Jean's pink blouse with lumps of clashing colours. Like a spattering of rain falling from the ceiling, the girls and tables looked like an artist's depiction of modern splatter painting. The girls took the whole incident lightly and made it a laughing matter. After wiping and scrubbing off what they could in the girls' washroom, back they trotted to the somewhat alarmed mothers to complete the rest of the first lesson. I decided to let Mrs. Chin and Betsy's mother do the talking and demonstration. Pandemonium I caused during the first lesson had taught me a lesson . . . one that was quite different from the ones that the other girls had learned during this baking lesson.

The second part of the baking class was carried out in a calm, orderly manner. My observation of the happy, engrossed looks on the girls' faces as we were taught the amazing techniques of cookie decorating, showed the satisfaction and enjoyment derived from this wonderful experience.

When the boys returned from the woodwork class, their chattering confirmed that they had learned a lot, though probably interesting, but not as much fun as we had, and probably not quite as amusing. We wanted to share the fruit of our labour, or rather the cookies of our hard work with the boys in our class. They weren't perfect by any means. We had already tried each other's baking. Even though some of the cookies didn't have quite enough sugar or had too much salt, and a few were on the burnt side, the girls were proud of their first attempt and achievement at baking. Expecting the plates of fancy, decorated cookies to disappear in no time, most of the boys surprisingly declined a second one. The only person to eat two of them was our teacher. So that the cookies wouldn't go to waste, we gave one to each of the teachers,

Mr. Lee and Mr. Harding who remarked how pretty the cookies looked and how scrumptious they tasted. There were a few for each of us to take home to our parents. Some of us even decided that we'd form a baking business when we got older. This was probably the third time I'd changed my mind as to what I wanted to be when I grew up.

Chapter Twenty-Three

One day I could no longer keep my silence. I shouted at Daddy Chen, took my sister's hand and burst out of the house shouting, "I'm going home!" After our altercation, I ended out back in his house. I don't remember the two times that I took my sister's hand and told her we were going home; perhaps I wanted to blot this from my mind, but my good friend on Charles St. told me a police car had come a couple times to pick us up and take my sister and me back to our home in the Chinese neighbourhood.

As months rolled by, I occupied myself with school activities and assignments, joining CGIT, joining the Chinese girls' drill team, playing with new friends, listening to music and radio programmes, practising the piano, and anything else that would help me pass the time and keep my mind off of where I'd like to be and how I could achieve this. I had attempted to change some of my ways, but there was always a missing piece in my childhood journey. In some ways it was like a puzzle that wasn't yet finished.

Little did I know that future events would

change our lives. Daddy Chen owned a restaurant in Vancouver so most days he was busy working there. Then he began spending more time at home. I didn't question him since I didn't speak to him anymore than I had to. And he didn't tell me why he was spending so much time at home instead of being at work. In a short time, he became bedridden. I soon realized something was not right, but still didn't ask questions. I walked by him each day, but didn't say anything. One day, Daddy Chen said, "Carly, come and talk to me." I stared at him for a minute, and without a word I walked away. Little did I know that he was dying of cancer. Whether this would have made a difference in my behaviour, I don't know. I was still the same me – proud, silent and stubborn.

During days when I was less active, I had ample time to think. I pondered on stories and lessons that I had learned at home and at Sunday School. It was one thing to hear God's word, but another to put the words into action. Words such as love, forgiveness, kindness, trust, kept popping into my cluttered, hazy head.

When my fogged mind became clearer, I realized the first thing I had to do. It was time to change my proud, stubborn nature, for the time being anyway, and show my humbler side. I tiptoed into the bedroom where Daddy Chen lay staring at the ceiling. I brought a small cup of homemade soup for him to drink. I could tell from the whiff that stung my nose, there were strong medicinal herbs in it. I helped him raise himself up against three pillows. As I held the cup to his mouth, his half-opened eyes widened and I noticed a slight shine in them. He uttered my name and took a couple sips of the soup which moistened his dry mouth. He mouthed, "Thank you", as he motioned it was time for him to lie back again. As he looked up at me with his heavy eyes, the words came blurting out of my mouth, "I'm sorry, Daddy Chen, for acting the way I did. I didn't mean to hurt you. I know I made some pretty mean remarks and appeared so uncaring when you became sick. I know you tried hard to be a loving father. Thank you for all the things you did for us. I know you only wanted what was best for your children. Thank you for being a good father." Daddy Chen smiled. Then with the expression of contentment, he closed his eyes and went to sleep. That day Daddy Chen peacefully passed away.

My feelings were ambivalent—sad and glad. I was sad that we had all faced bitter, unhappy times, for the uncharitable remarks I made and for being so unsympathetic when Daddy Chen became ill, but glad that I had realized my faults and made reconciliation with him.

When Chinese fathers or mothers die, the children wear black bands around their arms for a grieving period of one month. I remember going to the cemetery and bowing three times. I remember seeing Mom there. My sister and

I wore black bands around the sleeves of our gray coats during this time. I always felt self-conscious, thinking people were staring at us.

Chapter Twenty-Four

By this time Alex and I had become good friends. We both lived on opposite sides of Jackman Street. There were times we happened to bump into each other on the way to school so we'd chat along the way. We actually had a lot in common. I told Alex how I missed having a pet to which he replied that he had a German Shepherd named Roskee. After telling him we'd always had a cat or dog in our house he offered to stop by sometime and join them when he was walking Roskee and taking him to the nearby park. How could I not notice the enormous change I saw in this boy walking beside me. Alex even offered to carry some of my books when I had a heavy load. This Alex who seemed so mischievous, egotistical, smug and pompous when he first ran into me on the school playground, was a completely different person. He had become kind, considerate, and supportive. But then, maybe I appeared to be a different girl to him now. I realize that I wasn't quite as obstinate, cynical or judgemental, among other negative traits.

The school term would soon come to an end.

The grade six students had a choice of two junior high schools in the catchment area — on the west side was Thomas Jr. High and on the east side was Briteck Jr. High. My friends at Sir John Arnold School would be going to Briteck which is where I hoped to go even though it meant a long trek to and from school unless we took the streetcar. The grade sixes from Breymar had a choice of Briteck or Thomas. For them it would also be quite a distance. I hoped that Brenda would choose Briteck even though I'd heard that some of her friends were planning to go to the junior high on the westside. I also secretly wished that Alex would choose Briteck. One June day I happened to hear a group of boys talking about their summer holiday plans and where they'd be going in September. Douglas was certain that he'd be going to Thomas for two reasons; his father owned a business not far from there which means a ride for Douglas and there was good feedback from students who had attended the school. Bobby who lived near Douglas knew he could catch a ride with Bobby. It sounded perfect to him.

My hopes were dashed. Nobody or nothing dare break up this trio. They'd been friends for so long and depended on each other for support through thick and thin. It wasn't even fair of me to wish that one of them would leave the others. That was just plain selfish on my part. I would really miss my Beymar schoolmates, more than I'd ever thought. I hugged the girls that I wouldn't see next fall and shook hands with a few of the boys including Bobby and Douglas. I heard Bobby and Douglas cajoling Alex with a free ride to school and information advertising Thomas Jr. High's fantastic curriculum choices as extensive and the better of the two schools. Alex took a quick glance my way, then turned to talk to his buddies. As I waved to all of them, I was going to say my personal goodbye to Alex later. As I met Lin coming out the school door, we exited the schoolground slowly and quieter than usual. I didn't hear my sister's voice as she spoke. I was busy making a wish. Sunny day, sky so blue, let my wish today come true. Then I looked at Lin, took her hand, and we ambled on homeward.

My spirit rose when I remembered that there would be my old companions from Charles St. as well as those that I knew from Sir John Arnold Elementary moving on to junior high. They'd be going to Briteck Jr. High. I felt a little more at ease knowing I'd see familiar faces and have no difficulty feeling that I was again part of a group to which I had once belonged.

The last day of school came to a close. We bid farewell to all the teachers who had endured the year with the classes, some more challenging than others. Knowing I would never see these teachers who had made a significant impact on my life, I said my goodbyes to each of them, beginning with the principal, Mr. Harding, the vice-principal, Mr. Lee, and then to Mrs Lowe,

Miss Pollinger, and ending with Mr. Emmy. In a cheerfully sad tone I said, "Mr. Emmy, I'm glad you were our English teacher. I learned so much from you in your unique way of teaching us, and it was lots of fun, too. Thank you, from the bottom of my heart . . . I mean bottom of my pocket", as I reached down and pulled out a chocolate heart. "Oh, and if Mrs. Baker returns to Beymar next September, and you are still substituting, I hope you come to Briteck Jr. High." Mr. Emmy got in the last word this time. "Carly, you have been a very resourceful, witty child. I have a teaching position in the fall at Briteck Jr. High. If I ever feel at wits' end, I'll be sure to look for you." A sudden burst of laughter filled the air from a smiling teacher and a delighted student.

After Daddy Chen died there must have been another court hearing. We were told that my sister and I would be returning home to Mom and Dad—joyous words that I had wanted to hear for month. It had been a long year and a half since we'd been taken away. Now Soo had not only lost her husband but would also be losing two children. She had tried hard to be a good wife and mother. We couldn't blame her for what had happened.

We left Soo as friends, said a few kind words, and told her we would keep in touch with her. When we parted, Soo handed me two pieces of jade jewellery: a beautiful jade ring and a jade necklace. Jade is considered to be a powerful, lucky charm that brings harmony . . . Maybe this was Soo's way of saying "'I wish you good luck and much happiness' as you return to your home."

Chapter Twenty-Five

Just as Ms. M, the social worker had driven us to our new home in the Chinatown neighbourhood, she would be taking us back to the home we had been taken from almost two years ago—our home. Just as no words could express our deep thoughts when we left, on our arrival home at first there were just smiles on our faces, but very few words. My ears heard a sigh and the soft words of a familiar voice, one I had been yearning to hear for a long, long time. From my Mom's beaming face I heard a trembling but happy voice saying, "Carly, Lin, my two girls. You're home to stay." My wish had been granted; my prayers had been answered. Soon followed the grins, hugs, sobs, tears of joy streaming down our faces, laughter, and lots of chatter. Then happily and excitedly we all rushed towards the familiar house, my loving home where my sister and I belonged.

I thought to myself, "There was a loving God looking after us all this time after all." Inwardly I knew there is a purpose for all things, and somehow all things had worked together for good. My greatest wish that Lin and I would come back home was granted. When we left our home, I had begun my pleading heart with "Please, Lord . . ." Now with a joyful heart I was saying, "Thank you, Lord."

Everything and everybody was the same and yet different. Two years makes a huge difference in your appearance when you're a child. There's a change in your appearance as well as the qualities that make you who you are.

My east side friends were astonished as they crowded around me. I was at least three inches taller, a little heavier, had shorter, wavier hair, and after chatting with me, they noticed a certain air and tone that I didn't have before. It was as if I were a different person altogether. It didn't take many days for the group to realize I wasn't the identical girl who had left them almost two years ago. Previously I had been obstinate, determined, bossy, impatient, and slightly vain. Now there were signs of humility, contentment, patience, and compassion. But then, I'd only been home for a few days.

Billy had completely recovered from his injuries on the basketball court the day of the tournament between Beymar and Johnson. I was surprised to hear that he'd been keeping in touch with Alex since then. They both chatted on the phone regarding their basketball cards and were still exchanging cards among a group of them. Billy mentioned that Alex was inquiring about me and asking how I was adjusting to another change. Billy thought I was nearly my old self. There were the times though when I seemed so pensive and off in another world. Alex remarked that I'd been the same way at his school. I would drift off into a world of my own, a wishing world. Billy suggested that one day perhaps the three of us could get together to which I usually had a good excuse. Even though I wondered what Alex was up to during the summer months, seeing Alex and knowing it might be the last time our paths crossed would just make me feel worse; after all I'd have my friends at Briteck and he'd be making new friends at Thomas. So I occupied my time with my usual summer activities.

I was two years older so a neighbour asked if I could babysit her five year old while she worked at the Pan Tan Bakery on Main Street two days a week. It not only gave me a little extra spending money, but I was usually given two or three little cakes that were left over from the day. Those scrumptious little desserts made my mouth water. All the mini-cakes and pastries had different designs and were made up of layers of crisp puff pastry topped with a heavenly buttercream. I shared my good fortune with the rest of the family even if it was just a teeny bite since I knew we couldn't afford such a luxurious dessert. In my mind this decadent rich-tasting treat was for the rich. I wished I had more babysitting jobs. My wish was granted and I was busy looking after the children of two more families that lived within two blocks. If I earned enough money this summer, I planned to surprise my family with a huge box of Pan Tan's delicious desserts.

Chapter Twenty-Six

I had always kept in touch with Brenda. It seems we were always phoning one another exchanging the latest news in our neighbourhoods. The kids were either having fun with summer activities like summer camps, going on short vacations, looking after their younger brothers or sisters or doing odd jobs. Before Brenda left for a three-week summer camp at Lord Byng, she heard that Alex's PoPo had been sick. When she returned, her mom told Brenda the sad news that Alex's PoPo passed away. She hadn't seen or heard from Alex since and no one else seemed to know where he was. The last time Billy had talked to Alex was when their rendezvous was cancelled because of Alex's sick grandmother. Since then there were no returns to Billy's phone calls to Alex. I felt so badly. The time Alex needed a friend, no one was there. Bobby and Douglas were away at the same camp as Brenda, and I wasn't there when I could have and should have been. Poor Alex.

I immediately found Billy who was talking to the boy next door. After passing on the latest news he would try phoning Alex again and arrange to meet him, only this time I would be tagging along. There were so many unanswered questions. Where are you, Alex? What are you planning to do? Which school did you finally decided to enrol in this September? Carly and I are eager to see you. Can we help you in any way? The return phone call Billy and I were hoping for didn't occur.

The images I had of my farewells to my schoolmates appeared vividly in my mind. I saw myself saying goodbye to Bobby and Douglas. Then walking away with the intention of seeing Alex at least once more before the beginning of summer holidays never occurred with the sudden announcement and excitement that we'd be going back home. Feelings of regret prevailed. Rhetorically I said to myself, "Why hadn't I made the effort to share my mixed feelings with someone to whom I'd grown close? Why hadn't I told him how I appreciated having someone listen to my frustrations as we walked to school? Why hadn't I told him he was a very special friend who would be deeply missed? Why hadn't I told him all the great things I'd heard about Briteck and hoped I'd see him there? I wish I'd told him so many things . . . I wish, I wish, I wish."

Babysitting, swimming lessons, chumming with my friends, and a two-week holiday at White Rock in our trailer helped to occupy my mind for the remainder of the summer holidays. Noticing I wasn't always my perky self, my response that I'd had a hectic week seemed to satisfy the inquisitive.

This was the first time I was eager to begin the school year. Briteck was known for its strong academic programme, wide range of interesting courses, interesting extracurricular and noon-hour activities, and volunteer work in the community. All these in addition to meeting new teachers and kids would be a once in a lifetime experience for all of us.

About two and a half weeks before the big day Aila and I decided to ride our bicycles up and down the street. When we heard the tune of the ice cream truck, we turned around and whizzed back to my house. I jumped off my bike with gusto and hit my tailbone on the bicycle seat. As I cried out in pain, Aila came to my aid. Lending her shoulder for me to lean on, I hobbled towards my house. That was the end of my physical activities for the last two weeks of holidays as I lay on my side with a very sore bruised tailbone. The doctor had made a few suggestions: putting ice on the coccyx for a few days, taking aspirin, sitting on a doughnut cushion. I refused the first suggestion of ice but took an aspirin to ease the pain. When I was brave enough to sit up, I used an old cushion with a hole cut in the middle. Eventually I was able to sit down as long as I sat alternatively on each side of the buttocks.

I wasn't quite as eager to begin school now. There's no way I'd carry a doughnut shaped cushion around with me. I didn't think anyone would believe me if I carried an inflated tube around with me saying that I'd just come from an early lifeguard safety lesson and had nowhere to leave it except under my seat, my very sore seat. My excuse for limping was that I stopped a runaway shopping cart with my foot. Knowing these were downright lies, I thought it best to tell the truth. I fell off my bike was sort of the truth. I was excused from PE with a note saying that I had a misfortunate accident a couple of weeks ago and hopefully I'd be able to participate in the PE programme in the near future.

After following the doctor's orders, my tailbone healed much quicker than I was expecting. The pain had assuaged and the limp had become inconspicuous. I was ready to face the new challenge in September.

Chapter Twenty-Seven

For the first two weeks Aila's sister who was finishing her holidays was able to give us a ride to and from school. What a relief! My bottom and my feet needed to be broken in gently. I don't think either could handle more than the hours spent walking from room to room and sitting on the hard seats in the classroom which were probably meant to keep the students awake. I was grateful that there were always two or three girls and boys that I knew from my previous schools. When I found out Aila and I were in the same music and home economics classes we were both excited. Whenever I saw a boy with black hair, I'd take a second look with the hope that it was Alex. No such luck.

The second day I walked into my English teacher's room. I was extremely disappointed when I walked into the room only to find Miss Gravely. She was a gray-haired woman with her hair pulled back tightly into a bun. She continually pulled up a pair of gold-rimmed glasses that insisted on sliding down on her beak-like nose. Her dowdy clothes made her look even older, although to me her retirement days were not far away. Rumours were going around that she was a spinster who spent most of her evenings marking all the daily assignments she gave to her classes. I had only been in the room for half an hour and didn't hear any of her favourite descriptive words applied to students like banana toes, imbecile, or lazy daisy. I found out later that the rumours were started by a few of last year's troublemakers. Apparently, she was so strict that only three of her grade seven students had passed last year. Later I found out that the rumours were started by the three troublemakers who failed. All the other students in her classes passed.

The next day due to overcrowding there was a need for shuffling students in a few of the classes. One was the English class. A third one was formed to take the overload. Students whose last name began with A to L were moved to form a third English class. I took my load of books and walking down the corridor to our new room, I felt a light tap on my shoulder and the words "I'll take that load off of your shoulder." As I turned my head, there was Alex. Looking a little pale and tired, he explained the events of his summer. Listening to him attentively I managed to hold back the tears. Aware of my empathetic expression Alex quickly changed the subject. "You look great, Carly. I like your tan. You must have been doing a lot of outdoor activities. Did you do much swimming?" Here was Alex trying to lift my spirits when I was the one who should have been lifting his. I told him what a busy summer it had been for me. I also mentioned that Billy and I wanted to get together with him but weren't able to contact him. Alex told us that he had moved in with his aunt and uncle who lived about six blocks from the school. But he had already decided the last day at Beymar that this was the school for him. The day he looked my way as I said goodbye to Bobby and Douglas is the day he told his friends he wouldn't see them in September because he was going to enrol at Briteck. The day we didn't have a chance to say our goodbyes is the day he was planning to tell me of his decision. "In a way you helped me make my decision", he said shyly.

As we headed towards our rooms, I stopped at Room 209. "This is where I get off", I said. "I'll carry your books into the room", he said in a light-hearted manner. Then he set the books on my desk and instead of leaving he sat across the aisle from me. "This is where I get off, too", he chuckled. As our English teacher walked in, the class gave a whoop. There at the front of the class stood a handsome young teacher with curly hair and brown eyes. It was Mr. Emmy. After introducing himself to the class, Mr. Emmy looked at Alex and me. With a twinkle in his eye and enthusiasm in his voice he jokingly chortled, "I recognize two faces in this room. One belongs to a witty young girl; the other belongs to a bright young lad named Alex. I guess this year we have two smart alecks in the room." to which everyone joined in laughter.

I forgot all about my bruised tailbone. This had been one of the happiest days of my life. My wishes had come true and prayers that I had made over the past year had been answered. I had wished to be like the boomerang that had flown through the air only to return to its source. I had wished to be like the lucky horseshoe that landed on the peg; my attitude towards those who I thought had wronged me had gradually changed. I had developed deep bonds with a friend which I hope would continue over the years. If I hadn't moved to the Chinatown neighbourhood I would never have learned what it's like to live in a Chinese family setting, to learn about the Chinese culture, to have met new friends, and most of all to have met Alex. Now I'm home again with my loving family, caring friends, and challenging new school and life experiences. What more could I wish for?

Chapter Twenty-Eight

Because we were so busy with school activities, I with my drama and music club and Alex with his basketball practices, we didn't see one another except passing in the corridor or having a brief conversation in the English room before Mr. Emmy began the lesson. For some reason my insides felt different when I saw or spoke to him. It was like a chemical reaction when mixing two specific chemicals together. There was a feeling of direct combustion. I felt heated and full of energy whereas with other guys nothing occurred. Alex was not always easy to read so I was never absolutely sure how he felt about me or I about him until Cindy appeared.

Cindy was a new foreign exchange student from Hong Kong. She spoke English fluently but adjusting to a new environment was not easy. I should know. Cindy was a pretty girl with long black hair. She was tall for a Chinese girl and well poised. She was placed in a few of my classes so I tried to befriend her and make her as comfortable as possible in her new setting. Although her grammar was good, I noticed that she had trouble with a few of our common idioms and colloquial expressions. When we had a composition assignment, she was having some difficulty. During one class lesson Mr. Emmy asked that we pair up. Cindy asked Alex for assistance with which he politely consented. I didn't mind, but noticing that they were spending more time together, the green-eyed monster started to take over. I recall the large green dragon with its fiery tongue, but had never faced this new creature. I would try hard to ignore it. The following week I found out if it was possible.

Saturday was the day of the school Christmas bazaar. There would be all sorts of inexpensive knick-knacks to purchase as Christmas gifts for family and friends and for our secret pals at school: book marks, mugs, mini pencils or pencil crayons, character erasers, fridge magnets, notepads, candy canes; you name it. There was also a booth with a student selling Christmas raffle tickets. I thought at two for fifty cents that might make a good gift to add to Mom and Dad's presents. The winner would receive a surprise trip. My chances of winning were one in ten thousand but it was for a worthy cause so I purchased my tickets. In the bustling crowd I happened to run into several classmates but didn't see Alex. I heard someone mention that he had seen Alex but didn't have time to talk with him because Alex was heading to Cindy's house for the afternoon. I don't know which dropped first, my mouth or my heart. I closed my eyes for a moment hoping an image of the little green-monster wouldn't appear. When my eyes opened, Cindy stood before me. As I stared at her in bewilderment my mouth and eyes widened. Just as I was going to speak, she interrupted with, "I'm sorry, Carly. I invited a few special people to my house this afternoon as a thank you for their friendship. You were one of them. It was much easier to settle into my new school environment with the kindness of some of you. Jimmy apologized today for forgetting to tell you that you were invited to my party. I hope you're still able to come." I responded with a quick yes.

Then we both walked to her uncle's house together. Cindy lived about six blocks south west of the school. I hadn't been in the Richman area before but I heard it was an affluent neighbourhood. After walking passed the colossal houses with their striking architecture and enormous yards I understood why only the wealthy could possibly live in this dreamland. It was fun walking through it though. Then in an excited voice Cindy said, "Here we are." Behind the evergreen hedge was her aunt and uncle's house. It fit in with the gorgeous architecture of the other houses on the street. As we strolled along the beautifully landscaped yard with its brick path, I recognized some of the hardy flowers lining it. There were yellow mums, delicate looking snow drops, pansies and red cyclamen. We had some of those flowers in our flower beds at home. Other rare ornamental flowers I hadn't seen before. The spacious yard was dotted with pink, purple and red rhododendron bushes, holly bushes with lots of red berries as well as winter plum, Japanese maples and several yew and other coniferous trees. The tiny gnome, the lady bug, the brightly lit coloured lanterns and all the other garden sculptures and ornaments among the fairylike scene were like a dream, a winter paradise. With a gentle nudge on the shoulder, Cindy whispered, "Follow me." As we strolled through the arboretum my eyes gazed on three fallen fir trees which were purposely shaped to form a shelter, a sanctuary for a baby in a bundle of soft needles. Over the manger were angel figures. From them beamed dazzling lights. Next to the creche was a little stone wishing well embellished with tiny forest creatures. It reminded me of our Christmas play "Miracle in the Forest" which we'd be rehearsing the last two months except this was no play; this was the real thing, a miracle made possible all because of a certain friend.

When we arrived a few of the guests were already there. A few kids from other classes were chatting. Then I saw Alex who had just poured himself a glass of lemonade. When he spotted me, he came over to say hi. At that moment in walked Cindy's uncle, a gray-haired, business-like gentleman in a pinstripe suit. Our attention was gained by a clinking of a spoon on a rice bowl. Mr. Chan wished to thank us for our welcoming hospitality to his niece. She had thoroughly enjoyed her short stay in Canada but would be returning to Hong Kong during the Christmas holidays. You could tell by the sounds of disappointment by her school friends that she would be deeply missed. Then Cindy gave a short speech telling how she had enjoyed her days at Briteck and made us laugh when she told of a few humorous incidents that had occurred in the classroom and around the school during her time with us. As we mingled with each other, nibbling on the delicious appetizers, we took turns with our well wishes to Cindy on her return home. I wanted to tell Cindy that I should have spent much more time with her and hoped she'd return the following year as a foreign exchange student. Cindy pulled me aside away from the clamouring crowd. Secretly she told me that she was homesick. She belonged in Hong Kong with her family and other friends. She was especially anxious to see a certain someone who would be waiting for her. Cindy went on to say, "In some ways I'm like you, Carly. Coming to Canada has been an adventurous journey for me. I've learned so much, but now I'm ready to go home where I belong. There's a very special fellow waiting for me. At one time he was pretty obnoxious in order to get my attention. But now he's completely the opposite. He's the one for me. I guess I felt good talking and working with Alex because he reminded me so much of Kin. Alex told me a bit about you. I can tell the way he talks about you and that certain look he has when he sees you, that you're the one for him. Don't let him get away because of your stubbornness, Carly. He's a good catch." I gave Cindy a great big hug. "Thanks, Cindy, from the bottom of my heart. Thank you." We returned to the noisy room. Nobody noticed or turned their head except Alex who faced me. There was a certain gleam in his eyes as they met the sparkle in mine.

Chapter Twenty-Nine

I enjoyed my grade eight classes. Some were more challenging than others but I was willing to face those challenges even though it meant more work and studying. We had a study period which I put to good use and joined two extracurricular activities which included the school choir which was a mixture of female and male singers, the girls' ensemble consisting of eight singers, and the drama club which exposed students to the basics of theatre in an interactive, fun-filled environment. I enjoyed my choices since I had always loved music, and playing the role of another character would be a new experience for me. Performing in front of a crowd had never been my cup of tea so singing and acting would be good practice for me. My workload was filled to the brim. Every spare minute at school seemed to be taken up with rehearsals for the Christmas performances which would be upon us in a short three months. The two choirs would be practising two new songs Christmas songs in addition to variations of three familiar Christmas carols with a slight upbeat in a couple of them. I'm glad I wasn't in the band. I haven't heard or seen anyone sing, act, and play an instrument at the same time. I suppose there's a first time for everything, but that wasn't for me.

I recognized some of the kids who were in the band at Beymar. They must have practised a lot during the summer because they didn't sound at all like the ones who were in Mr. Hornsby's class in grades six and seven. I guess the ones who made the poor music teacher turn gray decided not to choose band as an elective. This year's band also included the string, percussion and wind instruments but somehow they were much more melodic in comparison to all the discording sounds I remember from last year.

The school choir was composed of singers who were divided into four sections: the soprano and alto for the females and the tenor and bass for the males. I was always more comfortable as an alto since my voice range could never hit the high notes without straining it and sounding like a timid mouse or howling cat. I had always wished I could hit the C an octave above the high C with the beauty and ease of a popular singer like Sarah Brightman, but for now my goal was to improve my singing skills as an alto. Reaching the F below middle C to the F above middle C was going to be enough of a challenge since there was a part in one of the musical pieces which required a harmonizing chord which would put me to the test. I would have to work extra hard to improve my comfort range of B below middle C and the B an octave above it. "Good luck", I wished myself.

I was envious of the girls' volleyball team which travelled to various schools to compete in the competitions. On the other hand, it would have been impossible trying to fit all these activities in my already too busy schedule and disastrous to the volleyball team. Luckily for them I didn't quite make the tryouts.

Tuesdays were choir practices and Thursdays were drama classes. Mr. Paichant was our drama teacher. He was small in stature, had slick brown hair, and entered the room with excellent deportment. He looked to me as if he could have been in his mid-forties. What I found striking about him was his hair which he combed every so often to keep each hair in place. I don't think it would have moved anyway with all the guck he must have slapped on it in the morning. He must have finished a tube of Brylcreem or a jar of Vaseline in a fortnight.

In my drama class there were two groups of students: one was the stage crew and the other the play cast of which I was part in the drama class. I learned a lot about acting, play production and stage work. The stage crew was also known as stagehands. They worked backstage with scenery, props and special effects in all the productions or performances. Their role was vital by knowing exactly where and when to move objects and scenery.

At our school there would be two culminating

performances showing the knowledge and skills absorbed by us during the year.

I had lots of practice expressing myself; just ask anyone who knew me. Doing it in front of a crowd as someone else was another thing. We learned to project our voices whether speaking in a loud or soft voice and the manner of the tone making it believable to the audience. At first, we put our knowledge to use while reading our short script. Memorizing the script would come later. We learned about interrelationship to other characters as we learned short skits and plays. We all thought this would be easy. Mr. Paichant had spent some time on theory and the history of theatre. Next came the practical part of the course. He was certain by now we were prepared for the next few classes in which we would demonstrate our talent by speaking short monologues. We listened attentively with the hopes that we would learn from each other. What began as an interesting lesson became more boring as each student took his turn. By the fifth monologue some of us were yawning and when it was my turn, I paused only to hear someone snoring. I wasn't the only one who heard this rude participant. "That will be all for today", announced Mr. Paichant effectively varying the elements of sound. With sighs of relief, we all scurried out of the room.

The next lesson was better, but not by much. We were each given one line of a short skit. Before memorizing the one line, the whole skit was read to us so we'd know the storyline. The first part of the skit went well. From then on, the whole skit plummeted. Either the wrong person would speak a line at the wrong time or someone would forget to come in and when they did come in, they forgot part of what they were to say. Since we were busy trying to remember our lines everyone completely forgot to express themselves in words and actions. Mr. Paichant had to come to our rescue, cueing us when it was our turn, starting us with our so-called memorized line, whispering loudly to remember our tone, speak louder, and whatever else was needed.

At the end of this lesson Mr. Paichant took out his handkerchief to wipe his brow, uttering the words of encouragement, "Things will improve on Thursday." By the expression of frustration on his face I think the words of encouragement were meant for himself, not for us.

Our next drama session with Mr. Paichant was anything but boring. He told us we were showing an improvement giving us suggestions as we continued repeating our lines with ways to convey our emotions, feelings, and thoughts to the audience. We worked hard on a combination of facial expression, gestures, and movements to create a certain effect. Not only Mr. Paichant but all of us could see how we had advanced since our first day.

It was unusually warm this day so someone opened a window near the stage which was a big mistake. Two big horse flies whizzed by some of the cast and decided to land on Mr. Paichant's head. That was the second mistake. They both landed on the surprised teacher's head. One slid on his slippery hair like an airplane trying to land on an oily runway. It skidded sideways and fell dangling from his right ear. The other fly was helplessly fluttering its wings as if it had fallen into quicksand only gooier. This is the first time I'd seen Mr. Paichant lose his composure.

He was shouting, "Get these repulsive insects off of me!" as he shook his head and arms in all directions. Someone yelled out, "Mr. Paichant is freaking out!" to which a bunch of us ran to his aid. Johnny hollered, "Get a newspaper. I'll swat it", to which Jenny, an animal lover shouted, "Don't you dare!" As he reached for some masking tape, Jenny snatched it out of his hand. Meanwhile Mr. Paichant was hooting, hollering, and dancing around to the buzzing of the flies. In all the turmoil I walked up to Mr. Paichant and calmly said, "Don't move." With a quick flick of my fingers, the fly on his ear flew away towards the window. Jimmy handed me a pair of chopsticks and I fished the other flapping fly out of the sticky mess. As Jimmy threw a glass of water at it, the second fly disappeared out the window. As poor bedraggled Mr. Paichant gained his composure and was about to speak to us, the principal at the back of the room remarked, "Mr Paichant, your work with the students is remarkable. I haven't seen such an impressive skit for a long time." As we looked at Mr. Paichant, he calmly said, "I think by your actions, my lesson on conveying our emotions, feelings and thoughts, was achieved today. You're all ready for the preparation of our Christmas production which will begin next week. Have a good weekend!"

Chapter Thirty

I really had empathy for some of my teachers. Teaching wasn't always the most rewarding job. Most of the teachers were industrious, committed, knowledgeable people who wanted to develop the potential in their pupils and change the negative attitudes of the few who seem to be occupying seats in order to keep them warm. School was a challenge for both teachers and students. Teaching was not a nine to three job as it appeared to some. There was always the necessary preparation for daily lessons, giving extra help to struggling students after school, taking tests home to be marked, and volunteering for extracurricular programmes. I later found out that many of our teachers had hidden talents or skills. Miss Harmon, the music teacher wrote the music for a song we'd be performing for our Christmas performance and Miss Gravely wrote the accompanying lyrics. Mr. Paichant had written the play for our Christmas performance, and Jenny, who was a former pupil at Beymar told me she'd seen a beautiful piece of art work at the art gallery by the now famous artist A.T. Scribbs. Just think, this teacher at Beymar was a famous artist who encouraged me to continue sketching when he jokingly told me my umbrella looked like a mushroom. It dawned on me that teachers can have a sense of humour, too. "I sure hope Mr. Paichant has one", I thought. "There are four weeks to go before Christmas holidays."

I've never seen a month go so fast. Here it is the evening for which it seems we'd been planning and preparing for since September. The night of the Christmas performance was incredible. The crowd was much larger than we had expected. We all had the jitters never acting in front of adults besides our teachers. As I peeked from behind the drawn stage curtains, my nerves settled a bit when I spied my mom, dad, and siblings seated in the front row. Next to them sat a friendly couple with whom they were chatting. As Alex looked over my shoulder, he noticed his aunt and uncle in the first row. "I'll introduce them to you later", he said excitedly. "Right now, all I can think about is my lines." All the classes had participated in making Christmas decorations which adorned the auditorium. As people flocked into the room, they heard a variety of Christmas music. Finally, when they were seated, the principal gave an opening speech, thanking the teachers and pupils who had worked so hard to make this night happen.

To get the audience into the Christmas spirit after singing "O Canada", the band played a couple familiar Christmas pieces. Then everyone sang some favourite Christmas Carols: Jingle Bells, White Christmas, Joy to the World, O Come All Ye Faithful, Rudolph the Red nosed Reindeer, and Deck the Halls. You could tell by the enthusiasm of the audience how much they were enjoying the evening. Then the lights grew dimmer. When everyone had quietened down, Mr. Paichant introduced himself, spoke a bit about the drama club and then introduced the cast in the production of "Miracle in the Christmas Forest".

It was our Christmas production of "Miracle in the Christmas Forest" written by Mr. Paichant and Miss Gravely. They chose to write a tale which might have been considered by some as a far-fetched tale. I liked fairy tales because the story always ended with "happily ever after".

I guess that's why I liked Mr. Paichant and Miss Gravely's tale about a little girl named Angel who wanted a Christmas tree for her poor family. As she wanders through the deep forest hoping to find a small tree, she is met by an old, hunchbacked woman who beckoned her to come as she cackled, "Hello, little child. Come closer so I can take a good look at you." A cool breeze swept through the dying trees whispering inaudible words. Becoming louder and stronger it began to howl, "Cunning old wretch, cunning old wretch. Watch out for the cunning old wretch!" Suddenly the old lady glared at Angel. She was a sorceress of some kind who had cast a spell on the trees making them lose their beautiful needles.

As the old witch gave Angel her evil look, the innocent child fell into a deep sleep. She dreamt of a peaceful night with stars shining over some fallen trees which formed a stable like shelter. In some soft grass lay a baby with bright rays of light surrounding him and tiny forest creatures singing songs of love. Angel felt the radiance travel through her body. As she woke from this dream, she spotted a young boy who took short walks through the woods. His name was Lexi. Noticing the withering trees, he brought a homemade potion hoping this would revive the falling greenery. As he eyed the spooky-looking haggard, he tossed the potion at her, changing the old lady into a kind, loving person and the withering firs into strong majestic trees. Somehow that little baby in the humble little shelter had magically filled the forest with the miracle of love. Among all the friendly forest creatures, fairies flew from branch to branch and elves stood on toadstools all joining in a Christmas song which had not been sung since the sorceress performed her evil magic.

Oh, we will sing of a tiny forest child
So sweet, so innocent, so mild,
Shining brightly on him the stars above
Granting the little one's wishes of peace, joy and love.

Now that the forest sorceress was filled with the miracle of love, she had a complete change of heart. The caring old woman promised to care for this babe who was lying on the soft needles and tend to the forest trees and creatures from then on. She sowed magic seeds which would grow trees, bushes and a vegetable garden so that the forest animals would have ample food. She promised to take care of the trees and animals just as they would provide and take care of her. From that time forward there would be hazelnut trees, apple trees, blueberry bushes and blackberry brambles which would provide food for the forest creatures. Pines, spruce and fir trees would be nourished and flourish, ready for children and their mothers and fathers when they came looking for the perfect tree to don their homes at Christmas time.

As the happy children waved goodbye to the kind-hearted old lady, the smiling young lad took the shy maiden's hand. The squirrels, bears, deer and birds led them out of the magical woodland together humming, whistling chirping and singing the forest Christmas song. Stepping out of their fairyland, Angel and Lexi who could be heard singing their new Christmas song were joined in the background by the school choir. Soon the throng of voices permeated the atmosphere with this new song of love.

The performance was truly a miracle. It went on for an hour and a half without a hitch. The audience was completely mesmerized. The cast did cast a spell on them as they watched a fairy tale come to life. When the performance ended the astonished onlookers applauded them with sounds expressing their approval. As the characters took their bows in turn, there were continual rounds of applause by the assembled spectators, ending with a standing ovation.

Mr. Janson, the principal, walked briskly to the front once again thanking the teachers, students, cast, stage crew, the volunteers; everyone who had made this wonderful production become a reality. Mr. Paichant and Miss Gravely who had created the fairy tale were applauded as they came forward to receive their gifts of gratitude. When Miss Gravely walked to the stage to accept the bouquet of flowers, I couldn't believe my eyes. This was the same woman who taught in the English classroom. Her hair in a chignon style and fashionable outfit made her look like a middle-aged model. Graciously she accepted the pink roses and Mr. Paichant with his usual poise received a book on the latest plays. Unable to keep his composure, he broke down and as his arms flew into the air, he effusively thanked the Drama Class, raving on about such an exceptionally talented group he had worked with this year. Looking at the cast he proudly said, "Tonight there was not only a miracle in the Christmas Forest, but there was a miracle on stage thanks to all of you!" The clapping and cheers continued until the lights became dimmer and we ended the evening singing Joy to the World, Silent Night, and then the darkness became bright with a flicker of the lights. Everyone joined hands and with great gusto our loud voices sang "We Wish You a Merry Christmas". What a beautiful way to end a perfect evening!

All the cast and singers ran up to their parents who were enjoying the refreshments. The repeated compliments of tonight's performance made us all grin with pride. Alex and I were surprised when we found that my family and his aunt and uncle had been sitting next to each other. I was embarrassed when my dad said, "So you're Alex. I was wondering who was making Carly's face light up." I knew Alex was just as embarrassed by the expression on his face when his aunt and uncle said, "I heard Alex and his chums joking about English being his favourite subject now because of a witty girl in his classroom. You wouldn't happen to know who she is, would you?" Fortunately, some of our classmates interrupted this sensitive conversation. They suggested we say our farewells to Cindy now since she'd be leaving on tomorrow's afternoon flight to Hong Kong. I excused myself and gave Cindy a big hug. With tears in my eyes I wished her a safe journey home, a happy time with her family, and hoped she would be back next year.

Chapter Thirty-One

At this time of the year we all look forward to the beautiful snowflakes falling gently to the ground. How peaceful they could look forming a winter wonderland on earth. But for those travelling in the sky the ice crystals could be ominous. According to the weather forecast a severe weather storm was predicted within twelve hours. There was an announcement of a possible shutdown of airports due to poor weather conditions. Cindy's plane had already departed and was two hours into the sky heading right into the blizzard. Those who knew she had left for Hong Kong listened anxiously to the news. Silently we prayed. I wished Cindy and her uncle had gotten stuck on the way to the airport and missed boarding the plane, and if they had gotten on the flight, I hoped they had already landed in Hong Kong. I guess it was hopeful wishing. I listened to the radio all day. There was no news about airplanes having problems due to the weather conditions which was good news.

After last night's restless sleep due to the excitement of our Christmas production, and today's fretting over Cindy, I was exhausted. As soon as my head hit the pillow I was in dreamland. The buzzing sound of the alarm clock woke me so that I wouldn't be late for church. I turned on the radio so I could hear the morning news while I hastily ate my toast and egg. The dreaded news that I didn't want to hear came on the eight o'clock news. I turned up the radio. The radio announcer repeated the news report. Flight 86 to Hong Kong which arrived at Kai Lak airport this morning was unable to land safely due to mechanical problems. Though there were no casualties, a few passengers had serious or minor injuries. We will keep you informed on the latest news report.

Soon the phones were ringing with the bad news. I stayed in all day mainly because cars were getting stuck on my street due to the deep snow. As I sat comfortably in my warm house, staring out the window at a winter wonderland, the fallen snowflakes may have looked beautiful, soft, warm, and glistening in our backyard but hard, biting and icy elsewhere. It depends how you look at it and from where.

We received a phone call from Uncle Ben's sister the following day. He asked her to pass on the good news that he and Cindy had a few bruises and were discharged from the hospital. As far as he knew, the other passengers would recover from their injuries. What a relief this was to hear the good news!

Our Christmas holidays were as busy as

ever with various events: attending practices for the children's Christmas programme depicting the first Christmas, helping Mom with the Christmas baking, shopping for presents for everyone, going carolling, socializing with my neighbourhood friends, attending the Christmas Day Service, helping out with our big turkey meal—everything that makes Christmas a special and joyful time of the year.

A few days before New Year's Eve I received an unexpected call from Cindy. What a great surprise! I'd been thinking about her and was wondering how she was enjoying her holidays. She thanked me for the Christmas card and little silk book mark I'd placed inside of it. She was well and excited. "Carly", she said eagerly, "Uncle Ben is making a quick short trip to Canada and wants you to come back with him." I couldn't believe my ears. "Cindy, that sounds wonderful and I'd love to see you, but I don't think it's possible." I didn't tell her that it would be too expensive, and I wouldn't want to ask my parents even though they'd be willing to sacrifice their hard earnings in order for me to make the trip. I thanked her for the invitation and said we'd keep in touch by mail.

Chapter Thirty-Two

Christmas holidays were over much too soon for all of us. The exciting month of December was shrouded by the back to reality dreary month of January. Once I returned to school and got back into the school routine, it wasn't so bad. Chatting with my school friends about our holiday experiences and coming school events cheered us up. Aila was always there for me but I think we all missed Cindy. The usual band of boys that hung around together were so engrossed that they didn't notice us as we headed to our classes at the other side of the long corridor.

Entering Mr. Emmy's room we were greeted with a warm, "Happy New Year, everyone! I hope you're ready for a new and exciting term." He heard loud sighs in reply. As his head turned towards Alex's desk he said, "My New Year's resolution is to outwit the wittiest students in my class, but one of them seems to be missing." I wondered where Alex was. It's strange that I hadn't heard from him during our break, really strange. Billy was a close friend of his. He must know where Alex is.

I caught up to Billy who was just exiting the room after the bell rang. Before I had a chance to ask him about Alex, he relayed the latest news on Alex's mishap combined with coming down with the flu which spoiled his entire Christmas holiday. Now I understood the reason I hadn't had at least a phone call from him during the two-week break. Apparently, Alex took his visiting cousin snowboarding at Grouse Mountain. His cousin, Kelly, not being familiar with the area went out of bounds. When Alex attempted to steer his cousin away from the No Trespassing area, he tripped on a sharp boulder, falling and injuring his leg. Kelly was unscathed but poor Alex ended out with a broken tibia. Feeling dizzy with a fever and the pain of a broken leg, I understood why rest in the comfort of a recliner with his leg elevated was all Alex asked for.

About a week later who showed up in Mr. Emmy's room leaning on a pair of crutches. He had a grin on his face in spite of the pain he must have been experiencing. "Hi, Mr. Emmy. Happy New Year", he said with a jaunty voice. "I went snowboarding on Grouse Mountain. I went head over heels after running into a sharp rock. It's a good thing I didn't land on my head. I landed on my tibia." I blurted out, "I guess the rock was sharper than you were." Mr. Emmy finished the dialogue with "I guess you just have ti bi a (tibia) sharper snowboarder, Alex." With that everybody laughed and applauded. Alex and I looked at each other with impish smiles. I think we read each other's minds. We were gearing up for the war of the wits.

As we gathered our books to leave the room my look of glee turned to one of sympathy as I apologized to Alex, "I'm sorry about your mishap. And to top it off you had to catch that nasty flu that was going around." Alex rebounded with, "Oh, it wasn't all that bad. I was treated like a king, being served all my meals. I was Alexander the Great for two weeks. My phone line was always busy with calls of well wishes from friends keeping me up on the latest news. They talked and I mostly listened except for a few croaky words due to my sore throat and laryngitis. Carly, I'm sorry I didn't even call you to wish you a Merry Christmas. I did pick up a little gift for you with my aunt's help. I was going to ask you to the New Year's Eve party at Billy's and give it to you then, but I still wasn't feeling up to crowds. Maybe for Valentine's Day we can get together. I hear one of the guys in my circle of friends has something up his sleeve."

The ringing of the bell for the beginning of the next class sounded. "We'd better get moving to our next class, Alex. Can I carry your books?" I chortled. Just then, one of his friends came up and grabbed his books. "Let's go, Alex. Mr. Boyle doesn't like us to be late for our science lab." I giggled, "The beakers won't be the only things boiling over." I always had to say the last word. "See you, Alex. Again, I'm sorry your mishap and misfortune made you miss school. I mean . . ." in sync we both chuckled, "Mr. Cool." With that Alex disappeared down the corridor, limping along with his crutches. I headed dreamily in the opposite direction not hearing the late bell. It was only January, but February was on my mind, February 14th.

Chapter Thirty-Three

Valentine's Day in junior high was a big event. In preparation for the special day in art class we created decorations for classroom doors and windows, in home economics the students made valentine cookies, in English class we studied the lives and poetry of some of the 18th century Romantic poets like Wordsworth, Coleridge, and Keats, poets who showed their individuality and creativity by writing short emotional and passionate poems about nature and the world around them

Although poetry can be written using a variety of forms: imagery, haiku, limerick, free verse, etc. we would only be discussing three or four of them this term. Mr. Emmy said we could take a vote on the type of poems to study. Being a democratic class, the majority decided on a rhyming poem. There was a vote on a jingle poem or a limerick. A limerick seemed to be the most appealing. Mr. Emmy described it as a humorous poem consisting of five lines. The first, second, and fifth lines have to have seven to ten syllables while rhyming and having the same rhythm. The third and fourth lines only have to have five to seven syllables, and have to rhyme with each other and have the same rhythm. There was one stipulation that Mr. Emmy required in these limericks. That was using words connected to Valentine's Day. We discussed rhyming words and since they were for Valentine's Day someone in the class decided we should rhyme words with romance. Although rhyming one-syllable words would have been simpler, thinking of words to rhyme with the second syllable of the word would also be permissible. A list of words was written on the chalkboard as students volunteered words: dance, lance, ants, prance, glance, chance, enhance. Then one student came up with the bright idea of putting the word 'no' before some of the "ance" words if they made sense.

In groups of four we worked vigorously on a Valentine's lyric.

We heard from two of the groups. The speaker for the first group recited his poem with emotion and expression. The last three words were shouted by the whole group.

There was a young lad named Beau Hance,
Who asked pretty Joan for a dance,
Beau got such a thrill
When she answered, "I will"
He shrilled and we yelled, "What a romance!"

There was a cheering with a round of applause.

Joey then presented his group's lyric. With confidence and articulation, he began:

There was a brave knight named Lotavance,
On his steed he'd prance with his lance,
Queen Guin gave a sigh
As Lotavance trotted by
'Twas the start of a nightly romance.

More cheers, hooting, and clapping filled the room.

There were three more groups to present their lyrics. The room seemed to be getting warmer and stuffier. Suddenly as if in a daze my brain went into overload. I didn't have a chance when my imagination took over.

Putting my brain to work, the words "smarty pants" appeared in bright red letters. "Oh no!" I thought. For sure both Mr. Emmy and the boy sitting across from me knew to whom I was referring. Just thinking of such a ludicrous thought was deplorable. As I grew deeper in thought, my chock-full imagination became more wild. I completely forgot I was in the English classroom.

Instead I found myself opening the doors to a courtroom, running and panting loudly towards the stern judge, he banged his gavel and with an irate voice cried out, "What's this panting all about?" to which I screamed, "No pants, no pants!" The jury couldn't figure out what I was shouting about and never did come to a guilty or innocent verdict. The confused judge just mumbled, "Mistrial, mistrial. If you promise not to enter or leave this courtroom with your silly panting, I will find you not guilty."

As I ran to the exit, gasping for fresh air, I yelled to the top of my lungs which just happened to coincide with Mr. Emmy's request for one more rhyming word for romance. As he said, "And what will be our final word to rhyme with romance?" with a hypnic jerk, I found myself yelling, "No pants!" to the roaring laughter of the uncontrollable class. Mr. Emmy in consternation ended the lesson on poetry and calmly said, "I think we've spent enough time on our poems for the day. You may finish them for homework. The next time you come to class we'll read a few selected short stories by our Romantic authors."

As he bent over to reach for his crutches, I grabbed Alex's books. As we approached the doorway, I knew Mr. Emmy would comment on my weird actions. "As usual, nobody ever falls asleep with you two unpredictable students in the class", he said with a casual smile. "I'll see you two on Friday with your finished assignments." I walked apologetically out of the room, muttering to myself, "I know what he's thinking but too polite to say, 'See you Mr. Cool and Miss Trial.'" Then I heard a voice trailing us. "Even teachers have a break. Carly, you might like to read your lyrics for your drama class. Break a leg. No offence, Alex."

Since February 14th fell on a Saturday, at school we celebrated Valentine's Day the day before. We had a Disney movie, a talent show, a short skit by the drama club. Cupcakes and Valentine cookies were handed out with a cherry flavoured drink. Valentine cards would be secretly slipped into a desk or a book. I found a little gift with a beautifully handmade card attached. On the front of the card were two little goats playing freely in a pasture among the bushes, weeds, and trees on the grass. Under the picture of the goats was the cute text "I'm not kidding around when I ask you to be my special valentine." That made me laugh. Inside was a creative poem expressing feelings of peace, joy, harmony, love, friendship. It made tears blur my sight. I call it the Alexander poem.

I unwrapped the attached gift. A tiny, transparent glass vase with two golden birds etched on it made my heart beat even faster. I hadn't realized that Alex was watching me from the doorway. "I'm speechless, Alex. Thank you for the lovely card and vase. Your poem was beautiful. I have a couple of things for you, too, but you'll have to go to Billy's party tomorrow to receive them." I didn't tell Alex that I had made some valentine's cookies which I was going to bring in a tin, but I burned half of them. The other little gift was a snowboard key chain.

Alex replied that he'd definitely be at Billy's on Saturday. With that, we smiled at each other and said, "I'll see you tomorrow."

Chapter Thirty-Four

Billy lived several doors down from my house. I had been to his house once before for a birthday do. You couldn't miss his large, beige house with a high yellow picket fence around it to keep his husky golden retriever in the yard. He had been trained to stay away from the flower beds which his father loved to tend. The purple crocus and white, yellow and pink narcissus were already beginning to bloom, brightening up the yard.

Mrs. Adams answered the door, giving us a friendly welcome. Then we followed her through a winding hallway which took us to a door leading down to the basement rec. room. This is where Billy and his friends sometimes hung out and played music. I knew most of Billy's friends and they weren't the type to wreck a rec. room. It really was a recreational room. Billy had a small amateur band which practised on the guitars and drums. There was also a media room where Billy and his chums watched DVD's. If things got a little loud, there would be a thump, thump, thump, on the floor warning Billy and his friends to turn down the volume. Since there were girls at this gathering, there wasn't a blaring sound from the TV or instruments; there was only the sound of fun and laughter.

We played Trivia Pursuit which belonged to Billy. Naturally he knew all the answers. Next, we played musical chairs. There was a couple of school friends who had just arrived from the Middle East. They had never played this game before so Billy explained, "This is a game with music and chairs. There is always one less chair than players. The music will start to play. When the music stops, if you fail to sit on a chair, you're eliminated. Another chair will be removed and the music begins to play again repeating the process until one player remains. That player is deemed the winner."

The music began and everyone moved around the circle of chairs in suspense, sometimes hesitating in front of a chair. When the music stopped, everyone raced for a chair, sometimes with two people trying to sit on the same chair. You could tell from the hilarious laughter that everyone was amused with the game. Finally, there were two people left and only one chair. When the music stopped, Brenda was as quick as a whip seating herself on the last chair while poor Tommy ended out sitting on the floor. While the crowd cheered for proud Brenda and roared with laughter at Tommy who pretended to sulk, a small box of valentine chocolates was presented to the winner.

A deep voice came from the top of the stairs, "Is anyone getting hungry? Come and get it!" In the dining room was a long table covered with a plastic tablecloth with cupid and little hearts. It was covered with plates of egg salad, ham and cheese, turkey, and genoa salami sandwiches. Some of the sandwiches had lettuce and tomatoes in them. There were even heart shaped grilled cheese sandwiches. On a silver platter were various hors d'oeuvres. I was hesitant to try the hot wings or jalapeno poppers but I tried the Asian beef skewers and salami roll-ups. They were absolutely delicious. Then Mr. and Mrs. Adams brought two trays with desserts. One had bowls of ice cream and jello, the other was a platter with chocolate cake topped with whipping cream and all kinds of cookies. I was full to the brim but managed to finish this fabulous feast with ice cream and jello. With glee all the boys zealously took the works. What a great party Billy put on! We thanked Billy for his amazing party and thanked Mr. and Mrs. Adams for providing the scrumptious food. They must have spent hours preparing the food for this special occasion. Before going out the door we each reiterated our thanks to the Adam's family.

Billy offered to walk me home. I graciously declined since Alex had already mentioned that he'd be heading that way. Also, it was an opportunity to give Alex the little gift that I had promised to him if he attended Billy's Saturday party. Billy watched us leave from his gateway. He looked somewhat bewildered and a bit jealous as he saw me hand Alex the wrapped gift. I turned my head towards Billy and said, "It's just a little belated gift that I wanted to give Alex after his accident. It's a get well wish for his healing leg." It was a fib, but some little lies are good lies if they make you feel better. I think this one made both fellows feel a little better.

Home and school life were pleasant but busy times. I still did a bit of babysitting to earn money and my marks were fairly good. There were only two months before Easter exams which meant studying for weekly tests to prepare for the big one. Also, my junior choir at church was practising two pieces which would be sung on Easter Sunday. We practised an hour and a half before the senior choir which would be singing a song on Good Friday and an Easter cantata on Easter Sunday. We had an extended holiday this year which meant a two-week school break.

I continued to communicate with Cindy by phone and mail. Usually it was Cindy who did the phoning. We kept our talks short because long distance calls were pretty expensive. I would write to her about my activities at home and school. Since she always asked about her school mates, including Billy and Alex, I also included my social life. Again, she wanted me to come to Hong Kong for a visit. I didn't say no to her, but I didn't say yes either. I just answered, "It just depends. I'm not sure if it will be this year, but I promise I'll get there someday" . . . I wish.

About two weeks later either my wish or a miracle occurred. The box that had been displayed at the Valentine's Day bazaar was brought to the stage. Mr. Janson, the principal, was going to reach into the box and pull out the name of the lucky winner who had entered the draw a couple weeks earlier. As he reached into the box filled with hundreds of entries, the hoping participants held their breaths as the smiling principal ardently echoed, "Carly Chen, Carly Chen you are the winner of our Valentine contest. You have won a fabulous trip to Hong Kong!" My hands rose to my rosy cheeks. I looked around and then stared at Mr. Janson in disbelief. I couldn't believe it. Me, Carly Chen, winning a dream trip to a Hong Kong. In awe, with a wide-opened mouth, I rose from my chair, a little shaken. Everyone clapped as I darted excitedly to the stage and up the steps where the smiling principal handed me my winning ticket. With joy I accepted the prize ticket and the voucher which was good for a ticket to Hong Kong. I could only imagine how happy Cindy would be when I told her I just might be able to visit her during my Easter break.

Chapter Thirty-Five

I booked my flight to my dream destination by Hong Kong Airlines which was suggested by Cindy's Uncle Ben. He had travelled back and forth with them several times and was always satisfied. The average non-stop flight time was about eleven and a half hours. I had never travelled such a long distance by plane before. I was fortunate to be seated near a window so on our departure I had a bird's eye view of the stately city, and the majestic snow-capped mountains and bodies of waters surrounding it. It was one of the most gorgeous, stunning panoramic views I'd ever cast my eyes on.

As the plane flew above the clouds, suddenly we were enclosed in a serene, blue environment with fluffy white clouds below. The humming of the plane lulled many of the passengers to sleep. Due to the adrenalin high from being high in the sky on a flight to Hong Kong I was unable to relax enough to be one of those lucky passengers. I brought along an informative book on Hong Kong which gave me some insight into its history, the people, their culture, and main attractions. According to the book, some of the popular attractions recommended were: Victoria Peak, the highest hill on Hong Kong island known for its skyline and waterfront view; Tsim Sha Tsui Promenade, a shopping and nightlife district; Lian Garden, a public park, leafy and tranquil with serene waters and rocks which head towards the red Zi Wu Bridge and the gorgeous, gold Pavilion of Absolute Perfection; the Po Lin Monastery, with the extraordinary 34 metre high bronze Tian Tan Buddha statue, and so much more.

It would be impossible to see even half of the attractions during my two-week stay in this densely populated urban centre and major port in south-eastern China. I decided to stretch my legs and walk up and down the aisle with a quick stop at the unoccupied lavatory. Then I hoped to take a nap before our arrival in Hong Kong. It was my usual bedtime at home but it would be morning in Hong Kong so a few winks would help. I don't think I'd slept an hour when the announcement came over the PA system by the captain that the commencement of the descent and approach to Hong Kong would be in approximately forty minutes. He also announced the local time and temperature at Hong Kong's airport. It was followed by an announcement from the flight attendant. "Ladies and gentlemen, as we start our descent, please make sure your seat backs and tray tables are in their full upright position. Make sure your seat belt is securely fastened and all carry-on luggage is stowed underneath the seat in front of you or in the overhead bins. Thank you."

By now I was becoming so groggy I could hardly keep my eyes opened to watch our descent as we became closer to the Kai Lak airport. I held my breath as the plane flew through skyscrapers and craggy mountains. They seemed so close I felt as if I could almost touch them. This was not as peaceful as our take off in Cathay Pacific from Vancouver. In fact, it was a hair-raising experience, but my body was both excited and exhausted. As I raised my tired body from the seat, eyes half closed, I sauntered down the aisle in the lineup. With a thank you as I passed the flight attendant at the exit door, though half dazed, my eyes spotted two familiar figures waving their hands and shouting my name. Cindy and her uncle were wildly trying to get my attention. Waving back with fervour, I knew jet lag was beginning to show signs. If only I'd changed my watch; if only I'd been able to fall asleep, enthusiasm for my wish would have been a dream come true at this precise moment. In Hong Kong it was 3 p.m. Sunday afternoon which meant it was 11 p.m. Saturday evening. I was completely confused and in a daze, but Cindy insisted on taking me to her house where I'd meet her parents. After that we took a short walk so I wouldn't drift off to sleep until their night time. Upon our return, we chatted about the events of the past two weeks, my airplane adventure, and made plans for tomorrow when I'd be more alert.

I had packed some souvenirs of Canada and other small items which I brought for Cindy, her parents, Uncle Ben, and a few extras just in case they were needed: souvenir tea spoons, smoked salmon, a jar of maple syrup, a Canadian calendar, tea towels, and Purdy's chocolates. Cindy's parents loved the tea towel with the dogwood emblem on it and the box of chocolates; Cindy was tickled with the charm bracelet which had little reminders of her visit to Vancouver dangling on the chain, and Uncle Ben was pleased with the smoked salmon which Cindy had mentioned was one of his favourite foods whenever he came to Vancouver.

That night I was surprised to catch a few hours of sleep. Wakened by the sound of goodbye to Cindy's dad, who was off to his business, and hearing the soft voices in the kitchen of Cindy and her mother, and the enticing smell of jook (congee), I stretched my arms and legs, dressed quickly, and wandered to the kitchen. "Jo shun, good morning", we said to each other. "And how was your night? I hope you had a good sleep", said Mrs. Lee My reply that it was wonderful and the bed and pillow were so soft and comfortable. Then we sat down to a hearty breakfast of Chinese porridge, ham, boiled eggs, and steamed stuffed buns. We had milk and Chinese tea with our meal. Cindy remarked, "My mom knows we need energy to do our shopping." After being stuffed, I thanked Cindy's mom for her hospitality and then we were on our way for the day. I was refreshed and a little more alert than yesterday.

I had already heard from my friend Cindy that Hong Kong was a densely populated urban centre among its impressive skyscrapers. Many of the tourists loved to shop here. Not only were there shops with fashions for every season but designer shops, and exclusive labels could be easily found at a bargain price. Besides clothing there were shops with silk products, artwork and almost any article you were looking for at an affordable price. Now I know why Cindy often looked as if she'd just stepped out of a fashion magazine.

Cindy suggested that we have lunch at a small restaurant called H & W over one block near the harbour. It was well known by the younger generation for its latest variety of savoury dim sum and delectable meals. Customers could gaze out the window at the remarkable scenery.

I was so caught up in all the fashions at such a reasonable price that I couldn't be lured away. While I continued to browse around the shop, Cindy headed towards the dock where we would meet in half an hour. Time travels so fast when you're enjoying yourself. I found the perfect blouse to match the slacks I'd previously bought. Noticing I was already five minutes late, I paid the clerk and dashed out of the shop heading up the street and then over one block.

Trying to rush through the crowded streets and becoming completely turned around with the little shops and soaring buildings, I began to panic. I asked several shoppers for directions but they didn't seem to understand me. Some of them stared in puzzlement and asked me to repeat myself. They spoke English but had difficulty understanding my Canadian English accent. Finally, a kind old gentleman pointed towards the harbour. In Mandarin, I smiled and said, "Tze, tze; tze tze" (thank you), then hurried through the shoppers, dodging the tourists who like me two hours ago were busy leisurely window shopping.

My panic abated when I found myself at the busy harbour with tourist ships and public transport ferries which were taking tourists for day trips across to Guangzhou, Macau or Shenzhen in mainland China. I looked around for eating places hoping to find Cindy but it was impossible because of the crowded area. I went to a toll booth to ask about restaurants by the harbour to no avail. One couple who was part of a group returning to the mainland noticed my bewilderment and offered to help. In her broken English the lady said, "You tourist. Can tell Canada accent. You go to Guangzhou? Nay hooy Guangdong, hi ma?" Then I understood what she said or thought I understood since I did know a little Cantonese. I proudly replied, "Ngo ba ba fun o kay Guangdong." In other words, I was attempting to tell them my father had been born in Canton. Unfortunately, they thought I was heading there to visit him. The friendly lady took my hand and we walked towards the ferry. Politely but frantically I said, "M hooy, m hooy. No go, no go", but she insisted. Meanwhile, noticing I didn't have a boarding pass, her husband quickly went to the booth and purchased a ticket for me. Between my thank you and no go we were pushed along onto the waiting ferry with all the other eager tourists and passengers who were rushing to get their window seats.

Mr. and Mrs. Lau, the friendly couple, met several friends and acquaintances from Guangdong, so we went our separate ways. My stomach told me it was time for lunch so I went to the cafeteria which featured a wide selection of hot and cold items. For those not hungry enough for a full meal, there was a variety of snacks to choose from: Asian sesame chicken salad, smoked salmon bagel, lobster croissant, BBQ pork handpies. Although they sounded delicious, I felt like a good old grilled cheese sandwich. I saw some cold meat sandwiches and then I spied a cheese sandwich. I happened to have a helper whose Chinese was better than her English. I knew the word bread in Cantonese was mainbow. But I wanted mine to be toasted so I pointed to the cheese sandwich. As the helper smiled and picked it up I said, "Mo, doh see, mo, doh see." I didn't want plain bread. No, I wanted it toasted. I forgot that you had to say the word doh see with a specific tone. I couldn't remember which went first; the high to low or low to high tone. Wouldn't you know it? I got mixed up and instead of saying that I wanted it toasted I told the helping lady, "Mind your own business", to which her smile quickly changed to a scowl. Unfortunately, I didn't get my grilled cheese sandwich so I took a BBQ pork hand pie which was very tasty.

From Hong Kong to Guangdong by ferry is approximately one hour and fifty minutes. I finished my lunch and returned to the passengers' section. My seat had been taken and there were no other empty seats on the second floor which meant the rest of the trip would be spent on the third floor. For the remainder of the voyage I managed to squeeze in between two large ladies carrying bulky bags. Listening to their loud chattering I missed the announcement that we would be disembarking in fifteen minutes. Either the elderly chatterboxes were hard of hearing or were waiting for the crowd to dwindle before they decided to rise, but I was beginning to get that feeling of anxiety again. Suddenly we were the only three left in the room. Moving the seniors' bags off of my lap, I sprung up from the seat and hurried down the stairs to the second floor where the end of the line of passengers were stepping onto the deck. I told the crew member who was holding the door that there were still two old ladies on the third floor. He casually answered, "Oh that's probably Mrs. Joe and Mrs. Lam. They ride on the ferry every Wednesday. It's free for Seniors so they like to ride back and forth from Hong Kong to Guangdong and back again just for the enjoyment, and they get to chat about old times, too."

I think I was the last one off the ferry. Mr. and Mrs. Lau were nowhere in sight. One of the ferry employees told me I could get one of the taxis that were lined up near the terminal which I did. I asked the driver to take me to a reasonable and reputable hotel that was in the centre of town. He dropped me off at the Guangdong Hotel located in the downtown city and near the beautiful YueXiu Mountain and the world-famous Dr. Sun Yat-sen Memorial Hall. The first thing I did when I reached the hotel was have a clerk phone to Hong Kong and get in touch with Cindy's uncle. Luckily, I had his business card tucked away in my pouch. There was an immediate response. I explained what had happened and was planning to return late the next day. I decided since I was here I might as well take in some of the attractions which were advertised in a brochure I was glancing at on the ferry.

Guangdong was a bustling, booming city with uniquely architectured buildings. As I was strolling along the streets, a voice came from a shop. Carly, Carly Chen. Is that you? I looked around to see who could be calling my name. Three men with their wives came up to me. They looked familiar but I couldn't quite place them. Then one of the fellows remarked, "You've grown taller and prettier than when we last saw you at your father's restaurant. I'm Jun. These are the cooks, Yook and Ho." A light bulb turned on in my head. "Now I remember you. You three were busy cooking at Daddy Chen's restaurant when I walked into the kitchen. Hi Jun, hi Yook, Hi Ho." I chuckled to myself when I said Hi ho. It made me think of Snow White and the Seven Dwarfs. Jun exclaimed, "What a nice surprise to see you here! You aren't here alone in this city, are you?" I explained the whole unfortunate episode to them and said I was planning to return to Hong Kong that day. Jun said, "This is our home city. We met your father here when we were kids." They all agreed that a young girl shouldn't be travelling alone in a big city far away from home. They would accompany me to a couple of sights in their home city and then ride back to Hong Kong with me on the ferry. I couldn't have been more relieved and I'm sure Cindy, her family and Uncle Ben would have been, too. I phoned and left another message with Cindy's parents. Then off we went as I hummed the tune to Carly and the three cooks . . . and their wives—Hi ho, hi ho, it's off on our holidays we go, throughout Guangdong, throughout Guangdong, hi ho, hi ho. It must have been a catchy tune because I was soon joined with whistling and humming.

That evening I returned to open arms in

Hong Kong. Cindy felt so badly, blaming herself for my situation to which I replied that it was all my fault. Cindy chuckled as she announced for the rest of the trip she wouldn't let me out of her sight even if it meant handcuffing me or crazy gluing me to her. Uncle Ben would be leaving in two days to attend an important business meeting in Vancouver which would coincide with my return flight home. Cindy and I did some quick shopping so I could find a few souvenirs to take home to my family and friends. I found some neat items in Hong Kong souvenir shops: fancy chopsticks, jade ornaments, lace work on white embroidery, coasters, bookmarks. I had already picked up a few things on our previous shopping trips.

On my final day in Hong Kong Cindy's parents and Uncle Ben planned a going away dinner at one of Cindy's favourite restaurants called the Yum Yum. It was a comical name but advertised the flavour enjoyed by the patrons. Much of the food on the menu was like that of a banquet I had attended, only it had a distinct uniqueness. The dinner began with an hors d'oeuvre followed by birds' nest soup, gai lan and Chinese mushrooms, scallops, rock cod, roasted chicken, snow peas and pork, and finally fried rice. I was so full it was hard to finish the lotus seed and lily soup with red beans. We knew the scrumptious feast was finished when slices of oranges and sweet cookies were served. I thanked Cindy's parents and Uncle Ben for the incredible and unforgettable evening. Our picture was taken by a restaurant photographer, one of a few that I had of my trip to Hong Kong. Uncle Ben waved good-bye as he said, "I'll see you at the airport tomorrow morning, Carly." To Cindy and her parents, he added, "See you in a few weeks." I couldn't believe this dream holiday was coming to an end. I phoned home once to tell my parents I was having a terrific time and to see how the family was managing without me . . . ha, ha. I told them when I was going to arrive home but they didn't have to worry because Uncle Ben's colleague was picking him up and would also give me a ride home. I hadn't even thought of Alex the last week and a half . . . well hardly ever.

The next day I woke up extra early knowing I'd be on my way home again. I had enjoyed my vacation in Hong Kong but was ready to return home. At the airport I gave Cindy and her parents a big hug and told them we would get together if they came to Vancouver. I would love to see them again. Uncle Ben added that we'd all get together again like old times to which everyone agreed with laughter.

Uncle Ben and I waved to Cindy and her parents as the plane began to take off. Ascending from the city and the flight home were much different from my experience flying to Hong Kong. Thinking of my many experiences of the last ten days, my eyes slowly closed and the droning sound of the plane soon drew me into a peaceful slumber.

After a few hours' sleep, I was wakened by the voice of the flight attendant who had a tray with meals. It wasn't at all what I expected. In comparison to the light meal and snacks I ate on my flight to Hong Kong, this was a full meal. But I had forgotten that Uncle Ben was able to get me a seat next to his in the business class section of the plane. Only knowing the economy class in an airplane, this was a delightful experience. I enjoyed the extra comfort of larger reclining seats with plenty of legroom and gourmet meals. Time on the flight seemed to whiz by as Uncle Ben and I chatted. I read a couple chapters in a book I'd purchased in Hong Kong, and took another nap. I remembered to set my watch back to Vancouver time with the hopes of avoiding jet lag. At least I would be able to sleep in my own bed when I returned home and had a couple of days to relax before returning to school.

Chapter Thirty-Six

Just as I had expected, my mom, dad, and siblings were overjoyed to see me as I was with them. They had met Uncle Ben briefly at a school benefit. I went on to tell them how wonderful he and Cindy's parents had been. After a few friendly words he was on his way. After the hugs and excitement, I answered all the questions about my trip and told of the wonderful hospitality given to me and a few experiences including the harrowing ones. I wasn't hungry. I just wanted to relax in my familiar setting. But first I had a few Hong Kong souvenirs and gifts to hand out to my family. There were lots of ooh's, aah's, and thanks. Mom and dad loved the beautiful silk cushion covers and jade ornaments; my sisters were tickled with the fans decorated with flowers and birds and my brother really liked the trendy coaster and key chain with pictures of racing cars. Everyone tried the Chinese cookies and candies which were a novelty. Besides the fan, I wanted to give my little sister something special, so later on I handed her a little silk gift box. When she opened it, there was a tiny angel in white embossed in jade on a gold necklace. With a loving look and big hug, she whispered a big thank you. As I placed the piece of jewellery around her neck I said, "This is for you, precious and delicate like my little sister." Then two tired, happy sisters went to sleep.

Though everyone was thrilled that I had such a good time and was home safely, I had a strange feeling that things were not quite right. For some reason the family seemed subdued. Though it was difficult, the daunting news was broken to me that Lin would be admitted to the hospital in a couple of days due to her weakening heart. The specialists would then decide what steps had to be taken. I couldn't believe my ears. I had been enjoying my holidays while my younger sister had been plagued with heart problems; yet she always remained cheerful and positive. As usual, she was a shining example for me with her strong faith when it was supposed to be the other way around.

While Lin was in the hospital, Mom would go early in the morning and stay until evening. With the rest of the family taking turns and Lin's friends and other visitors dropping in, Lin hardly had time to write her letter to her older sister in Calgary or to read the magazines or books that were given to her. She seemed extra cheerful and, in my eyes, stronger. I was sure she would be home again in a few days. Then the dreaded news that Lin had passed away was broken to me by Aila's older sister Meda. The shocking news stunned me. I couldn't believe that my sister was gone. I didn't want to believe she was gone. I asked myself over and over again, "Why, why?" Over the years I had wished so many times that Lin's heart would be healthy. I prayed earnestly that the specialists would help her. Why didn't God answer my prayers? I walked slowly to the window and saw a police car in front of our house and dad's car behind it. Mom and dad walked solemnly into the house where they repeated Meda's sad news. After leaving the hospital dad was so despondent that he was stopped by a police car for driving so erratically. When the police office heard the sad news of Mom and Dad's daughter's sudden death, the kind officer replied, "Sir, just follow me. I'll guide you home."

I'm sure a parent's worst nightmare would be the death of a child. Yet Mom and dad in their agony and sorrow remained calmer than I did. They reminded me that Lin was happy in heaven and one day we would see her again. Their strength, comfort and peace could only have come from their strong faith in the Lord. If only I had relied on my faith instead of my stubborn self, I wouldn't have been so miserable.

The Celebration of Life service for Lin was held at our church. It was a beautiful service with Lin's favourite songs, a couple close friends told of experiences with Lin which made us laugh and the pastor spoke comforting words which did relieve me of some of my misery. All of my friends including Alex were at the funeral service. During the refreshments we were given condolences by those attending and Alex mentioned that he would talk to me in a few days.

I returned to school a week later even though I wasn't myself yet. My teachers and friends noticed that I wasn't my usual witty self and my marks had dropped in some of the subjects. I didn't feel like participating in my usual extracurricular activities and usually headed home immediately after the bell not feeling like talking with anyone. As I headed down the street with a long trek before me, a familiar voice called, "Wait for me!" which I didn't hear being busy in thought. A gentle nudge drew me out of my trance. I looked up to see an empathetic face. There beside me stood Alex. He spoke to me calmly knowing I was still going through an emotional time. Listening to him speak of the tragedy he had experienced with his family's accident and the grieving and healing time almost made me feel guilty. Alex had the support of several people including his two buddies. I realized that there were several caring people who were willing to give me support during my bereavement, too; one of them was Alex.

There were two months of school left before the year was completed. The days were longer brighter and warmer which helped raise the spirits. The beautiful pink cherry blossoms and chirping of the birds filled me with a serenity that I hadn't felt for some time. I also continued to have short walks and short talks with Alex during and after school. There was no way I could get away with moping or my sullen attitude with all the support I was getting from those closest to me. My marks had improved again and even Mr. Emmy remarked that I was back to my old self. He said, "Keep that Chen up . . . I mean keep that chin up." I couldn't let him have the last word so I replied, "Good old Mr. Emmy . . . I mean, good, (clearing my throat) Mr. Emmy." "Same old Carly", he chanted back. With a friendly gesture of the head signalling an "okay, you outsmarted me", I walked out with Alex, both of us with grins on our faces.

Chapter Thirty-Seven

Two major events would be squeezed into May and the beginning of June: the interschool basketball championship, and a field trip to Victoria. Both Alex and Billy spent much of their time practising with the team which would be competing against Thomas Jr. High in the west end. They were the team's top players. The name Thomas Jr. High sounded familiar and then I realized that it was the school Alex's former school pals Douglas and Bobby attended. The three of them still kept in touch occasionally. They were all busy with school and social activities besides meeting new friends and having other interests. I was hoping the game would be played at our school so that I'd have a chance to see Douglas and Bobby again. My wish came true. Briteck and Douglas would have their first tournament the first week in May. Both teams were exceptional so it would be an exciting game. This time I would be able to cheer from the bleachers with the other spectators instead of being a cheerleader. I didn't even think of trying out as a cheerleader since I was already busy with the choir and drama club. The big day came and a large crowd of Briteck students were on the stands rooting for the home team. The cheerleaders chanted their home song for Briteck and everyone joined in. The players on both teams showed their incredible skills: bouncing, passing, defending, and shooting. Both teams scored sometimes a few points ahead of the other team, sometimes tied. By the end of the game Billy took the last shot winning the game for us. The boisterous spectators raised the roof with their applauding, cheers, throwing up their hats and singing the basketball cheer for Britecks unbeatable basketball team as they lined up and shook the hands of their opposing team. After the game, I ran down to greet Douglas and Bobby who were chatting with Alex. It was like old times, almost like old times. Before leaving, the guys said, "We'll get together again during the summer, just like old times." Alex and I replied, "Just like old times."

The day before the long weekend would be our field trip to Victoria. The grade seven classes with their teachers and parent volunteers excitedly boarded the school buses. Before the buses were on the way to the ferry terminal, after simmering down and giving our attention, Mrs. Harrison repeated complete instructions on appropriate behaviour and to stay with our teacher, assigned partner and the class at all times.

The ferry was packed with school students

that day. I think two other schools had the same idea as ours. Luckily Mrs. Harrison had mentioned we would be sitting on the first deck so if anyone thought they were lost, they were to go to the gift shop on that floor. Aila, Brenda, and I found double seats by the window. It was a beautiful day for a ferry ride with a blue sky and cool breeze. As we sailed through the strait Brenda remarked on the remote homes in the distance. We figured they belonged to wealthy, retired folks who wanted to get away from the crowds and busy life they'd spent over the years. They could watch the loaded ferries with their binoculars if they ever got bored.

While we were busy chatting, a large, smug-looking girl came up to us. Behind her were three other girls. I didn't recognize any of them because they weren't from Briteck. They must have taken body building classes from the looks of them. The large girl said snappily, "Hey, you're in our seats! We just got up for a pop and you snatched them!" With a startled look, I replied, "I'm sorry but these seats were empty when we came here and there was nothing on any of them to tell us they were occupied." One of the girls threw a bag of chips on my lap and shouted, "They are now!" As they snickered, I rose from my seat, annoyed; I lashed out with, "Now just a minute", at which point a guy showed up and sat in my seat. To avoid any further altercation, Brenda and Aila grabbed their jackets and decided to yield. Unfortunately, my obstinate nature sprang into action. "Listen, Mr. big bad wolf. Why don't you and the three pigs go back to building your houses? Then you can all use the rest of your hot air to blow them down." Me and my big mouth.

I had almost started an all-out brawl when my knight in shining armour showed up on the scene to find out what all the commotion was about. He just happened to be holding a cup of hot chocolate in his hand. When the bulky guy defending the smug-looking girl turned around quickly, he knocked the hot chocolate out of Alex's hand. "Ouch!" he yelled as the drink splattered on his bare arms. By then students from both schools were looking on. Some were prodding us on. A ferry employee and teachers from both schools showed up just in time before the volcano erupted. I said the four bullies had caused the confrontation and the four bullies accused Alex and me of the clash.

The six of us were set in separate rooms and isolated from everybody on the ferry for the remainder of the trip. I was extremely upset to hear that we would be disciplined by not continuing the rest of the field trip in Victoria. It was bad enough that I'd miss our tour of the Royal Museum and Wax Museum among other things, but poor Alex who happened to be in the wrong place at the wrong time was being punished unfairly. About fifteen minutes before we were to disembark, two of the teachers entered the small room. We were told to board our bus with the other students. I figured we'd be sitting in the bus while all the other students were enjoying the attractions. Then we heard the unexpected news. We would be enjoying the field trip with the rest of our group. Several people including passengers, students, and a teacher witnessed the whole episode. What a relief! We had lots to talk about on our bus trip home, not only about the attractions in Victoria, but also about the main attraction on the ferry.

When we returned to school, news of the episode on the ferry had already circulated. We were like front page news. There was also the rumour going around that Mr. Emmy was leaving our school at the end of the year. I couldn't believe my ears. We had one more class with Mr. Emmy. Only if I heard it from his mouth would I accept the rumour to be true. We had a quick summary of what had been taught the last term and told to study hard before our final exam the following week. Mr. Emmy told us he had enjoyed teaching our class and this was a great school. We should be proud of it. He ended by saying, "Good luck on your exam. Good luck in the future. I hope we run across paths again."

I was puzzled as to why Mr. Emmy was leaving. I sure hope it wasn't because I was such a smart aleck. The question was like a burr on my mind. I guess great minds think alike because Alex was also wondering why Mr. Emmy had chosen to transfer. We decided to meet him after school. As we rushed to Room 209 Mr. Emmy was just walking out the door with some papers. "Mr. Emmy, we'd like to speak with you", Alex said with a glum look. Noticing the expression on our faces he replied seriously, "I'll be right back. Have a seat", as he pointed to two chairs by his desk. Alex offered to do the talking. When he returned Mr. Emmy asked, "And what can I do for you sombre looking students? I hear you two are not only smart alecks but troublemakers, too. I guess you were bored on board." He was the only one who chuckled at the last remark. Alex started off with thanking Mr. Emmy for being such a good English teacher and wondering why he was leaving. I interrupted by saying, "I hope it's not because of something we've done." Mr. Emmy replied, "Of course not. Just the opposite. You two have made this class more interesting and challenging. Because of your remarks, more students in the class started to participate. Both of you have been a pleasure to teach."

Then Mr. Emmy told us he'd been offered a position at the university as an English instructor, a position he couldn't refuse. Upon hearing this, we were relieved, happy and gave our congratulations to Mr. Emmy. It would be the university's gain but our loss, for now. I didn't reveal that Alex and I had planned to attend the same university in a few years. So Mr. Emmy was not rid of us yet. He'd better be on his toes or put on his running shoes because he was bound to run across us some time in the future, near or far.

The saying "time goes faster as you get older" must be true. I'm only thirteen and don't know what happened to the first two terms of grade nine. I continued with my usual school routine and joined the school choir and drama club again. To my list I decided to join the running group that Billy belonged to. I finally gave into his persuasive reasons. I didn't need to lose weight like Billy did but running would be a healthy activity and could be fun. It didn't take long for me to realize that it was a strenuous exercise, too. We met twice a month on Saturdays. My aim was to eventually run five kilometres in less than five minutes. This was going to be a big challenge for me but I figured with determination I would manage. My main reason for joining the running club was to prepare for the upcoming marathon "Heartbeat". Donations would go towards heart research. I wish the latest discovery had been two years earlier. Maybe Lin would still be with me, physically I mean. Billy wanted to lose a few more pounds so Aila and I sometimes had company walking and jogging to and from school.

Chapter Thirty-Eight

This year I felt comfortable at Briteck, knowing the routine and the majority of kids in my classes. I recognized most of the teachers but a few were new. When I walked to R209, I had a feeling that someone was missing. Mr. Emmy wasn't there to greet his new students at the door. Instead a tall young man greeted us with a pleasant smile. When everyone had been seated, our new teacher introduced himself. "Hi, everyone. My name is Mr. Chatty, but I'll try not to talk too much." There were a few snickers. As he turned to write the topic of discussion for this lesson, someone gave a little tug on my hair. Startled I said, "Ouch!" Without turning his head, Mr. Chatty announced, "This is my first year in a junior high class. Some of my teaching methods might seem a bit foolhardy, but no fooling around. If there are any smart alecks in this class, be on your toes." After turning around, he added, "I have eyes in the back of my head." After hearing his lecture mingled with his wit, I figured he must have had Mr. Emmy as an instructor. This might not be such a boring class after all.

Mr. Chatty covered a variety of topics during the year. He introduced us to the literature and styles of different authors with their stories and poems. We reviewed grammar rules and learned techniques and skills when writing a composition or essay. These were presented in a serious way often with Mr. Chatty's added humour. Alex and I would sometimes return Mr. Chatty's comments with wit but not as often as the previous year. One of our big assignments was writing about a person who had left an impression on us, someone who had been a major influence in our life. I wrote about my sister Lin. Alex wrote about Mr. Emmy. Mr. Chatty was pleased with the compositions written by the grade nines. We also had a wish box which was filled by the students in Mr. Chatty's classes. May was the time for field trips. Mr. Chatty made the surprise announcement that the English classes would be going on a field trip to a place which would fulfil the wish of two students. He read some of the wishes of students which were hilariously impossible: I wish I could go to the moon in a space capsule; I wish I could go to Disneyland; I wish I could take a trip around the world. For those students, keep on wishing and dreaming. Then he said, "But we're all going to the university where we'll tour the campus and stop at the library and various buildings. We will also go to the Faculty of Education building where we will be met by one of my former instructors and your former

English teacher, Mr. Emmy." It was a wish come true. Visiting our witty English teacher, now a witty instructor was truly a wish come true.

The Friday before the May long weekend our school bus was loaded with excited students, eager to tour the university grounds. We began by touring the Museum of Anthropology with its renowned displays of world arts and cultures, with a special emphasis on the First Nations peoples and other cultural communities . . . followed by a stroll through the beautiful Nitobe Memorial Gardens. We found a quiet place where we could rest for a few minutes and eat our bagged lunches. After being refreshed we headed for the Faculty of Education building where we were invited to meet Mr. Emmy. A group of education students were just departing the busy building. We were led through the hallway to a large assembly room where Mr. Emmy was standing. As he stepped down from the podium to greet us, he gave us a hearty welcome and shook Mr. Chatty's hand with the words, "Good to see you again." As he looked my way he added with a smile and wink, "Hope those two aren't causing you any trouble." Then he came towards Alex and me saying, "You told me I'd better be on my toes because you were coming. I had to wear my platform shoes because my toes were sore. But I brought my running shoes along in case my feet got tired." Everyone laughed. "Same old Mr. Emmy", Alex said. I whispered to Mr.

Emmy, "Except I see tufts of gray hair." It was so good to see Mr. Emmy. As the school bus pulled up, I thought this unforgettable day had ended much too soon. Before we left, Alex and I rushed back to Mr. Emmy to say our goodbyes. Mr. Emmy and Mr. Chatty were finishing their conversation and shaking hands once more. I hadn't realized that the papers in Mr. Emmy's hands were copies of the compositions our class had written. Alex's composition about Mr. Emmy and our wishes that we would see him again at the university were among them. I won't forget the last words Mr. Emmy spoke to us. He said, "You two bright and witty students are highlights of my teaching career. I can't imagine either of you wit out (without) each other."

Chapter Thirty-Nine

Just as I had dozed off for what seems only a few minutes ago, I opened my eyes to find myself sitting in my cosy recliner. It took a second or two to realize the childhood events that embossed my vivid dream were times of a bygone era. With a gentle touch and the smell of a fresh cup of tea, I heard the familiar words, "It's time for our afternoon pick me up . . . a cup of tea for you and me. Yours is without sugar of course because you're sweet enough, Carly." With a sing song voice, I added, "Don't forget the cream." As he handed me the cream pitcher, I gave him my Carly smile. Pouring the thick yellowish liquid from the pitcher into his cup of tea, in a loving and sincere tone I said, "After all, Alex, I did get the cream of the crop."

At that precise moment, something popped up from the toaster. We clinked our cups together and said, "A toast to Mr. Emmy."

Mr. Emmy was not only an excellent teacher with a good memory but also a very observant one. He wasn't kidding when he told us he had eyes in the back of his head. He knew what the future held for us when he implied, "I can't imagine you two wit out (without) each other."

With the two of us under one roof Mr. Emmy knew wit in (within) the house there would always be happiness. He also remembered me once saying my favourite stories always ended with "happily ever after".

Epilogue

Though this childhood experience seemed heartless and fruitless at the time, pondering on it, I have become wiser and more understanding. I realize that a parent's love for their children is given in various ways, and this love is shown through words and actions not always understood by the children.

I have had the opportunity of being part of two worlds, of being immersed into two cultures which helped to mould me into who I am today. I am a proud Chinese Canadian girl with all the trimmings. What more could I ask for?

Acknowledgements

In memory of my loving mother and father, Jake and Annie, who were the inspiration for this story. Their shining example of a strong faith, thoughtfulness, compassion, respectfulness, patience, strength, courage, and sacrificial unconditional love had a strong influence on me as well as an impact on others who knew them.

In memory of my loving husband, Howard, who was always supportive and encouraging during the years of raising our children (Lillian [deceased], Chris, and Mark) together as I continued to teach and take UBC courses in order to complete my Bachelor of Education Degree plus another year to receive my ESL Certificate. My husband's example was passed on to our two thoughtful, caring sons to whom I am grateful for all their time and help.

I am grateful for the many fun experiences shared with my sisters—Eileen (married to Gerry), Lorraine, Shirley, and Lily—and my brother Jack, who is my only living sibling.

Thank you, to my dear supportive friend, Laila, with whom I spent many happy hours.

Thank you, also, to Doreen Brust Johnson, an author who referred Rivershore Books to me and gave me tips on writing a book.

To all my readers, I hope this story engages you with my writing, reminding you of your many childhood experiences, and that it appeals to your emotions through moments of laughter as well as sadness. I do enjoy using humour through a play on words. Laughter is good for the soul. I have found that behind a cloud there is always a silver lining.

Relax with a mug of hot chocolate and enjoy "Witty Carly's Wishes".

Rivershore Books

www.rivershorebooks.com
info@rivershorebooks.com
www.facebook.com/rivershore.books
www.twitter.com/rivershorebooks
blog.rivershorebooks.com
forum.rivershorebooks.com